CRITICAL ACCLAIM

This collection of fiction by poet Mansour Noorbakhsh, illuminates memories of moments lived in Iran. Each tale weaves vivid threads of reality creating a sensorial, living tapestry with its unique scents, sounds and cinematic sights of people and landscapes. Like the butterfly in its homonymous story, Powdery Wings will leave an indelible mark of its powder in your heart. This collection brings us to the essence of what it means to be human. Each story beautifully captures the experiences of love, loss, desperation, alienation, belonging and hope of people living within oppressive political confines, yet all the while transcending them with their universal humanity.

> — *Josie Di Sciascio-Andrews Author of seven collections of poetry and two non-fiction books. Her work appears in various journals and anthologies in Canada and internationally, among which: Canadian Literature, The Malahat Review, Descant, The Canada Literary Review. Has won an international prize in Rome's Citta Del Galateo Contest.*

In this exquisite collection of flash fiction, we enter a universe of emotions and insights that captures the essence of the human soul. Mansour Noorbakhsh's lens of keen observation explores the complexities of relationships, the desire for freedom, the profound depths of grief, and the struggle of the immigrant experience. With lyrical prose that offers poignant reflections on life, each story is a gem, transporting us across borders and cultures.

> — *Peta-Gaye Nash is the author of two short story collections, I Too Hear the Drums, Stories (2010) and Told Ya! Stories (2024). She is the recipient of the Mississauga Arts Council Awards for established literary art (2022).*

Streets, people, and houses. All in black and white, without shadows or additional color. But the pictures were perfect enough to show the essence of each scene undeniably. By this sentence from the writer in the third story I believe we can identify the theme of the book. There is life in these stories, the life of a humanity distracted by the daily frenzy, so much so that sometimes we don't notice the needs of others, as a relative, a friend, an old acquaintance, and as an migrant. The stories talk about love and migration, war, and freedom and one of the characters says, "freedom and life reproduction are interrelated". There are prejudices and the struggle to overcome stereotypes because "We all, regardless of our religion, are generally against free living and self-expression. That's the problem." The writer questions the future, and it is not obvious that technology can improve our lives if empathy and listening are lacking. Mansour Noorbakhsh does not provide answers but tells the present and the past in a flowing, conversational, current style. It is just automatic to find oneself in his stories.

> — *Claudia Piccinno, Italian Poet, and teacher. Author of Implicit published by Fara editore in 2023, and 50 other anthologies. She is the editor of Istanbul Gazette and the Turkish magazine Papirus. Her books have been translated into English, and other languages. Claudia Piccinno lives in Castel Maggiore near Bologna, where she has received the civic award for cultural merit.*

Stories by Mansour Noorbakhsh are little gems inviting us to the world of his memories through flash fiction pieces. They open doors to interesting worlds, full of seemingly small, everyday events but raising important questions that everyone should think about. Worlds worth visiting, a book worth reading many times.

> — *Neža Vilhelm, poet and translator from English and German languages, living in Slovenia, author of a collection of poems entitled Sotto Voce (2023).*

POWDERY WINGS

POWDERY WINGS

Stories of Immigration

by

Mansour Noorbakhsh

Library and Archives Canada Cataloguing in Publication

Title: Powdery wings : stories of immigration / by Mansour Noorbakhsh.

Names: Noorbakhsh, Mansour, author.

Identifiers: Canadiana (print) 20240305043
Canadiana (ebook) 20240305086

ISBN 9781771617680 (softcover) | ISBN 9781771617703 (EPUB)
ISBN 9781771617697 (PDF) | ISBN 9781771617710 (Kindle)

Subjects: LCGFT: Short stories.

Classification: LCC PS8627.O685 P69 2024
DDC C813/.6—dc23

Published by Mosaic Press, Oakville, Ontario, Canada, 2024.
MOSAIC PRESS, Publishers
www.Mosaic-Press.com
Copyright © Mansour Noorbakhsh 2024

Printed and bound in Canada.

ONTARIO ARTS COUNCIL
CONSEIL DES ARTS DE L'ONTARIO
an Ontario government agency
un organisme du gouvernement de l'Ontario

Funded by the Government of Canada
Financé par le gouvernement du Canada

Canada

ONTARIO
CREATES

MOSAIC PRESS
1252 Speers Road, Units 1 & 2, Oakville, Ontario, L6L 2X4 (905)-825-2130
info@mosaic-press.com • www.mosaic-press.com

To my companions in the journey,
my wife **Farah**
and our children, **Aida** and **Saeed**.

CONTENTS

ACKNOWLEDGEMENTS

Special thanks to Richard Harrison for his detailed editing, and my gratitude to Giovanna Riccio, Stephen Kent Roney, and Peta-Gaye Nash for their comments that encouraged me make this book ready for publication.

Thanks to Elizabeth Barnes and the weekly prompt project organized by her which, since 2020, inspired me write the first draft of some of these stories.

Thanks to Howard Aster and Mosaic Press for their kind attention to this book.

The first version of some of the stories in this book have appeared in WordCity Lit (https://wordcitylit.ca).

Mansour Noorbakhsh

PREFACE

Whatever the cost of freedom, it is not as heavy as tolerating oppression, injustice, and dictatorship. What you certainly lose by living under a dictatorship is your creativity.

Immigration has always been an attempt to save one's free will. But no matter what, such attempts only happen through tremendous changes that come with some degree of uncertainty and random consequences. To survive random consequences, creativity is not an option, but a must.

We move with our imaginations, we change with our mixed feelings, and pursue our intuitions. Therefore, we need to communicate with other people because creativity craves connection. For the immigrant, language barriers and the difference between mindsets often causes confusion. But inevitably, intentionally or unintentionally, we change as we try to overcome the challenges. But new challenges always appear, and satisfying one need raises another. Sometimes we notice how we change, but sometimes we are too busy with our daily work to understand the trend of our metamorphosis, what is happening to our body, our taste, our feelings. For me, living as an immigrant has been a bit like playing backgammon; within each step that we take to improve our situation, we toss our dice and move our pieces to new points, and whether successful or unsuccessful in our goal, we settle in a new place, both physically and mentally.

The fiction collected in this book addresses some less visible effects of immigration that could happen HERE, THERE, or ELSEWHERE, like the chapters of this book. These stories talk about the intuitions that move us toward a new place, our communication with people of different cultures, and finally our settlement as the result of all the random or designed steps we have taken. My life has taught me that we never find the right path to walk until we have explored many different options. But exploring different options leads to many trials that remind us of our limited lifetime, and, even if they fulfill one of our great expectations, deny many others.

And finally, in the way that all fictions are our attempts to tell the truth without truth's details, these stories are fiction, and any similarity between the names and events in this book and real names and events is completely coincidental.

Mansour Noorbakhsh
Toronto, 2024

MY CHILDHOOD RUNS AHEAD OF MY POETRY

Bear with me my feelings
till we both pass through,
our imaginations made wild
by silence and
the darkness of our way.

My childhood runs ahead of my poetry.

I'm not worried per se,
I just need your presence.

All seedlings are worthy,
even if not all of them fulfill
the promise of fruit.

What could be more futile
than expecting mutual understanding
from the dialogue of shadows?

Happiness happens in a common attempt
that only begins with a shared wish.

Mansour Noorbakhsh

I
HERE

POWDERY WINGS

I have already mentioned that some years ago I used to work in a small factory located in a poor neighourhood in the south of Tehran. The factory was close to a large oil refinery plant and a large cemetery. My home was in a wealthy neighborhood uptown. The streets were not very different between the two places, but everything else was.

I am not fond of driving, especially long distances. I called a taxi agency close to my home every morning to take me to my workplace and at the end of day, I called another agency close to that factory to take me back. A whole year long, I repeatedly made this trip.

A few drivers worked in each agency, so each day of the week one of those drivers came with his own car. Sometimes it happened that a new driver came for that trip only and did not come back. I presumed he moved to another place or had been hired somewhere else and hopefully was not struck with illness or some other misfortunes.

What we talked about during each trip was different depending on the driver and the direction. The drivers of each direction had some differences in their ages, habits and so on. Most of the drivers from the north-town agency were middle aged, retired men. Their conversations focused on illnesses like back pain, knee pain, and inflation or how to manage their income.

The drivers from the south-town agency were almost the opposite—mostly young men, many of them jobless, hopeful to become educated, wealthy, and sometimes suffering from a breakup because of an unstable income and social position. Those who never reappeared to drive me home likely faced such struggles or misfortunes. Did I say some drivers just came for one trip and disappeared after that? Yes, it happened.

One incident stuck with me. One afternoon on a hot summer day, a very young man came with his car to drive me home.

He was a new driver, well dressed, shaven, with neatly combed hair. It was one of those boring days when the sun's rays scorched that godforsaken oil refinery and the cemetery alongside it. I don't remember how our conversation started. It was clearly not a two-sided conversation. He was probably talking to himself most of the time and didn't need an audience to actually hear him out; he needed me to help him aspire to more.

He recounted how he had finally found his mother who was living in Denmark. At one of the Internet Cafés established around the city in those days, he had been sending emails to someone he presumed was his mother, having never seen her. He had been raised by his father in early childhood, then later by his uncle or aunt. (It was hard for me in this heat to keep track of all the details). He seemed deeply sad, but he was pretending to be happy because he had access to the internet and was self-assured and educated enough to send and receive emails. He talked about moving to Denmark as if it were next door. I remained mute, totally mute at that point and unable to join the conversation.

Do you remember when we spotted a butterfly and tried to catch it? We had to hold our breath and avoid making any noise, worried about losing the butterfly. Then the butterfly got scared and flew away as always. Conflicted with my inner thoughts and feelings at that moment, I was afraid of saying the wrong thing and ruining his dreams.

We left the oil refinery that was close to the cemetery behind, and we had almost reached my place. He was talking about how he was sure about the future and his mother in Denmark when suddenly, his car rattled, slowed down, and stopped in the street. Those godforsaken cars. I'm not even sure how they were able to get around the city in those cars. Left with no other choice, we jumped out of the car and together we pushed it to the curb. He had to call a mechanic. He was going to call another taxi for the rest of my trip. I paid him and after a warm thank you, I declined and said I'd like to walk the rest of the way. Although we were still a bit far from my home, it was possible to walk. After a few steps I turned, I don't know why, but I turned, then saw that he was walking desperately around his car, looking downward. My last memory is of him kicking his car tire angrily.

P.S. Do you remember those butterflies that you pinned on a cardboard and said we should not touch? One day I tried to catch one of them with two fingers, like when we were trying to catch them in the garden. Although I held my breath and moved my fingers very carefully, I noticed that the wing of the butterfly had changed to a powder that only stained my fingers.

DUSTED

Many years after my father's death, I found myself again in the village where my father had been a teacher and the principal of the school. The village was now almost completely uninhabited, populated only with old and barren palm trees, and a stream that was not going to any field. Whether it became an abandoned village because of an earthquake that happened many years ago or because of the attraction of modern cities or a long devastating war, was impossible to say; however, it was now deserted and looked more like an ancient village than the bustling one it once was. Yet I needed to get an official letter from one of the offices in this village before I applied for my passport to leave the country. Official letters are always needed even from an office in an uninhabited village.

When I arrived at our old house, the house I had left before my fifth year, Karim was still there, now old, and lonely. He had been a worker in this house and was still living there. People thought he was crazy, mentally deficient. But my father hired him to help Karim and his family. Even though my father also thought Karim had some learning problems, he strongly believed in educating everyone.

My father had been forced to leave his job for some reason that I was not able to understand. We left the village and Karim stayed there. Many years later I realized that my grandma and my father often sent Karim money. I remembered that we left the village in my jobless father's old jeep, moving anxiously toward Shiraz and then to Tehran. Now here I was again, needing paperwork to prove my own identity, and anxious with many worries about my security and not having enough money.

Karim remembered me, my father, and my mother. And my grandma too, who Karim used to call Madam. Karim opened the door and kindly welcomed me in. He did not know that Madam had died, and my father and mother too.

6

Old with downcast eyes, Karim talked with long pauses between his softly spoken words. He gazed into the middle distance, but it was obvious that he was not looking at his audience. I had to wait until evening because there was no car or bus to take me back before 8 pm. I talked to Karim and sat in the courtyard of the old house on an old wooden bench.

While we were talking, a mild earthquake shook the earth and the decayed building. Karim got up like someone who was going to do something, like someone with purpose.

"Don't be afraid, Karim," I said. "It wasn't that dangerous."

"I'm going...under...that palm tree...tonight...until morning." Karin said, staring with narrowed eyes, as though viewing a movie inside his head.

"Why?" I asked.

Stare and ponder... Stare and ponder. "It will rain fresh dates." Karim said. "That night it rained fresh dates too...fresh dates... the smell of dates... glistening...in the light of the lantern."

I was going to ask which night but remembered that a few nights after we left this house for Shiraz, there had been an earthquake in the village.

Karim continued, "She and I were going there...that night." He pointed to the courtyard and the palm tree. "When the earth trembled...the walls throbbed...we were walking to that palm tree." I assumed that Karim was talking about a girl who came to our house to babysit my newborn sister.

Staring and pausing as if nobody else was present, Karim strolled through his memories. "...she had a lantern in her hand... our shadows were moving together on the trees...on the walls... she said...hold the lantern, but don't come closer...don't come... she started to dance...under that palm tree...the lantern in my hand was dancing too".

Simultaneously Karim's hand was swinging like the pendulum of an old clock. I assumed that he was revisiting memories, and his actions reinforced it.

"She said stay there," Karim continued, "...and she was dancing...dancing and...dancing...I didn't go closer...and

suddenly the earth and the walls trembled…and the palm…
trees…and fresh dates…were falling…rain of fresh dates….the
odour of fresh dates…fresh leaves…she cried…cried…I rushed
closer… she was seated by that tree…I said let's go to the house…
she cried…we cannot…we will stay here tonight…there were
shouts and cries from afar…I said why do you cry?…I like rain of
fresh dates… rain of fresh dates on your hair… your hair smells
fresh…she said tomorrow… you'll…cry too." I assumed that girl
had known about the war and the ongoing attacks.

I was looking at Karim, paralyzed, stunned. I didn't know what
to say, so I smiled instead. I decided to try to calm down Karim's
fear of earthquakes, and asked, "hey, Karim, have you ever been
in love?"

Karim turned nervously, as if he had lost or forgotten something
and had to come back for it. He paced and stopped. Paced again.
Then he rushed toward the other side of the building where an
old kitchen was. He said, "Yes…here please…I have to give it
back to you…it's yours…Madam said to keep them clean…I kept
everywhere… clean."

Karim was right, everywhere was clean just as my grandma had
taught him.

Karim walked fast toward the old kitchen and again asked me
to join him. Long paces and staring into the middle distance with
fixed eyes like a blind man.

In the old kitchen with the fireplace made of adobe that had
seen no flame or any smell of food for many years, Karim looked
around carefully as if he was doing something illegal, and said,
"come…" and then he removed one adobe from the wall of the
fireplace. He took out a tin, a tin like an old gasoline container.
It had been cut and formed into a box, bigger than a shoe box.
Karim opened it and said, "It's yours…I kept them here…and
nobody knows…but Madam said I have to keep them safe…till
your father comes back…now…you are back…yours…"

I looked at the box. There were some magazines and newspapers.
I recognized my father's picture taken in his youth, and his name
written under a poem on the first page. I quickly looked at it.

It was a poem about freedom, and about good things for everyone, a sort of revolutionary poem. I turned back to Karim who was looking at the picture of a singer and dancer on the same page of that magazine. A quarter of the page was about the announcement of her show every night at a cabaret in Tehran. He looked at the picture of the smiling girl who was looking directly at the camera. She had curly hair and stood with one hand on her hip and the other hand slightly raised.

I gave up looking at any of the other magazines. I thought how strange it was that all these magazines should be compiled in a deformed gasoline container with the poems of a fired teacher who had a strong belief in educating everyone, and an advertisement for a club or lottery ticket. I went back to Karim who was still looking at the advertisement for a dancer.

"Do you know her?" I asked.

"Yes … she…was dancing…that night…"

"The night of earthquake?"

"Yes …" said Karim.

"Are you sure? She has never been here. She died many years ago." I looked at Karim who was now gazing at the wall. Not exactly at the wall. He stared with unfocussed eyes, looking nowhere, at nothing.

"Yes, she was…she is…her…herself…" he said.

It was close to 8 p.m. when we left the house. Karim said, "won't you…take this…box with you? It is yours."

"No, you keep it. You will keep it better than me. Much better than me, Karim."

We arrived at the bus station on the corner of the square on the other side of the village close to the road.

I got on the bus. Sank into the chair. Tired. Puzzled. When the driver pulled out, I waved to Karim who was still waiting for the departure of the bus, as if it was his duty to send me back safely.

When I turned and looked at Karim, I saw him looking nowhere, into the distance with the lantern swinging in his hand periodically.

AN OLD "NO PHOTOGRAPHY" SIGN

When I was six years old, we moved far away to a new city because of my dad's job. Those days, my dad had a camera. The type of camera with a leather cover and a long strap for carrying it around the neck or over shoulder of the photographer. The films my dad used to buy for his camera were as big as my palm. A thick paper covered the entire strip of film. One side of that paper was black, and the other side red with some words on it. When my dad gave that film to a photography shop to print the photos, sometimes the paper cover of film was given to me, and I used to play with it. Not many toys were easily available at that time. I was using it as a spiral-cone shaped telescope to pretend I could see distant things. Exactly how my dad had taught me. And sometimes I used that spiral-cone shaped paper as a trumpet to echo my voice.

One afternoon in late summer or early fall, Dad and I drove around the suburbs. Dad was going to take some photos of me in nature. With his camera in his old jeep, we set off. A street near to our house was close to some fields. We got out of the car and walked around, and Dad took a few photos. Then we ran to the other side of the road where some long hills were left without any grass. Some broken fragmented barbed wires had been installed around a small building as an office. My dad asked me to climb a small hill and he seated himself on the ground to take a photo of me as if I was flying in the sky. The wind was blowing, howling in our ears, and ruffling our clothes and hair. The effect of the wind was to make the photo exciting. My dad was about to take a photo when an old man came out of the office and shouted at us.

"You are not allowed to take a photo here."

"Why?" my dad replied.

"Don't you see the sign?"

"What sign?"

"That sign."

The old man pointed to a very old sign that was installed on the ground close to the broken barbed wires. The sign was rusted, a circular metal bolted to another rusted stand installed on the ground, a little way from us. A picture of a camera, but not like my dad's, had been drawn in the middle of a red circle with a crossed red line from one side of the circle to the other side. That old, rusted sign was to warn everyone that photography was prohibited in that area. The sign was so old that the colors and shapes were barely recognizable.

My dad laughed and said: "That sign? That's a nasty heritage from WWII, don't you know how long has passed since WWII? At that time this area had probably been an army base. And certainly, a base for a foreign army." Then my dad started to explain WWII and how Iran was occupied by foreign armies although Iran was not the partner of any countries in that war. Some years later, when I learned to read, I was able to learn the history as well as hear about the agony of wartime from elderly people. But in that moment, the old man interrupted my dad and said, "Listen, I know you are a teacher but I'm not your student and this is not your history class." My dad wanted to argue that this sign was useless today, but the old man insisted, "If I did not know you, I would have confiscated your camera."

I was not able to figure out what was going on, but I felt agitated. My dad stole a glance at me and while he was putting his camera in its leather cover, he said, "all right, I will obey that old sign," and sardonically insisted, "that old sign." The old man started to walk back to his office and turned and looked at us again and again to ensure that we were not attempting to take any photos in that area. We walked down that little hill. My dad laughed nervously and said something about rules, signs, and people which I couldn't understand. I felt ashamed and agitated for not being able to help him. He was silent and walking nervously. I looked at him and asked, "when will you give me the thick cover paper of your film?" I felt successful because my question not only made him laugh loudly but he tried to joke. "They will arrest you...hahaha...they will take your telescope...hahaha..."

I started to laugh and run away. I was repeatedly saying, "Then I will run away...hahaha." We were laughing and running toward my dad's old jeep. He was laughing and running after me, pretending he had fallen behind. The wind was blowing hard, disturbing our hair and our clothes, and howling in our ears. I was running faster, turning back to watch my dad. Then suddenly I saw that the old, rusted sign was rattling, shaking in the wind. As if a monster was following us, roaring, and laughing. Dad was still laughing and running after me with opened arms to catch me, mocking the old man, "Then they will arrest you...hahaha... they will confiscate your telescope ...hahaha..." And the rusted sign rattled monstrously in the wind.

WHO BLINKS FIRST?

It was all my fault. I encouraged him to apply for the contest. There were two months left of the school year. We were in grade eleven at the time. Bahram was new to this high school like me, and he was probably new to this city too. My family and I had come to the suburbs of Tehran in my dad's old jeep two years before. This was in 1983 during Iran-Iraq wartime, when my dad accepted his new job. Both of us – Bahram and I – were strangers to this school, therefore we became close friends from the beginning of the school year. We were not too close to the other students. Bahram was usually a silent boy occupied with drawing pictures on scrap papers like old magazines and newspapers in his free time. He was very fast at sketching. He was not using anything other than a single pencil — whatever its colour — rather than using coloured pencils. Although it seemed as if he was just doodling rapidly, he could draw pictures perfectly of what he had seen. Streets, people, and houses. All in black and white, without shadows or additional color. But the pictures were perfect enough to show the essence of each scene.

One day during recess, when we were chit chatting, Bahram drew my portrait on a scrap piece of newspaper. As always, he drew very fast with astonishing results. I could see my face in two separate areas. He had blackened one part, and the other part of the paper was left without any pencil spot on it. After seeing that portrait of me which Bahram had drawn for his own amusement, I said, "let's make something good…let's make a wall newspaper."

The wall newspaper was a large white cardboard that students designed with their writings and drawings. It was popular in schools at that time. A wall newspaper could also be adorned with pictures from magazines. Sometimes students were allowed to install their wall newspaper on the wall of a classroom or a corridor.

Bahram smiled as if he didn't take me seriously. But I insisted and tried to convince him that he was talented. His answer was

13

still a sardonic smile. I asked him, "How did you learn this? Did you take any classes?"

"No, no learning material or classes at all. What a strange question you asked! Have you ever seen any book or a painting class for how to draw on old newspapers?" answered Bahram with a laugh.

"But how did you learn that?" I insisted, repeating my question.

"I learned from beholding the night sky," Bahram replied and laughed again.

"Are you teasing me?" I asked.

"No, I'm serious. When I was a little child, my dad was working in another city. In the summer nights my mom and I used to sleep on the rooftop. We were living in a small city near Kerman before my mom passed away. I looked at the stars while she told me stories about them, or she sang lullabies. I was not able to memorize the name of constellations or remember all the stories of my early childhood. But even at that time, I was able to see how the stars or Moon had become distinguishable by the darkness around them without any additional lines. They were blinking in the depth of darkness."

Having his talent shining on a wall newspaper seemed even more exciting now. "Let's go to the office and get permission for a wall newspaper," I said as we started walking toward the office. But in the front of the office before we entered, we noticed that a painting contest would be coming to our district soon, and the selected student at our school would have an opportunity to attend other contests, and eventually a cross-country contest.

"Now, there you go. It's your time to show your talent," I said with a victorious laugh. Bahram was still not interested. I felt he was somehow shy or scared. But my feeling was to insist again and again to help him come out of his sad solitary state. After he agreed to participate in the contest, he was told by the office that he had to submit some sample drawings for the first run of the selection. The due date was close and there was not enough time to prepare new drawings. I was quite confident that Bahram could pick some of the drawings from what he already had in his personal collection. I assured him that there was no other student as talented in our school and probably in the entire city to compete with him. In fact, I was right, there was no other student with such talent. "Feel free to submit my portrait too." I said with a loud laugh. But Bahram just smiled.

The next day, a collection of Bahram's drawings on scrap paper was ready for submission. We reviewed them together. All of them were wonderful. A picture of our school building with a big bell on the entrance corridor. Bahram's dad and other workers working on the railroad, students on the playground, a beggar, and a bakery close to Bahram's home. He had cut them perfectly and neatly and had put all of them in a folder with his name on it. We were confident about submitting the folder to the office. We walked toward the office happily. I stopped at the entrance, and he went inside to submit his folder to teachers. We both had been nervously happy and anxiously confident about the result. The following day, Bahram was called to the office. I laughed and said, "Here you go!" He went to the office while I waited for him in the corridor. I expected him to come back quickly, but unexpectedly it took a long time.

He came back after almost thirty minutes, agitated and exhausted. I wondered what had happened. I asked him, but he was not calm enough to answer me. It was hard to ask him again, but I couldn't wait. It was obvious he was uncomfortable talking about what happened in the office. We were silent despite boiling in hell till the end of day. When we left school to go home, he noticed my worried look, as if I were asking again, "*What happened? Tell me.*" He broke his silence, and muttered some words, "Teachers were angry, maybe scared too. They asked me why I blackened some words from the speech of the leader of Revolution, and some other important news in my drawings. They thought I had done it on purpose. But I didn't even notice the words when I was doodling on the newspaper. You know, I'm just doing it to calm myself. To show what I can see. Words are not my interest. The teachers tore up all my drawings. Then they threw them in the garbage bin and shouting that I should never do that again."

15

WHERE WE GO!

"We are mocking each other. We are mocking nature. That's all we do our entire lives. I don't like mocking others. I don't like mocking nature. Where we go!" That's what my friend said while we were seated on the bench of a park. He used to repeat that phrase a lot. "Where we go!" Regardless of whether it fits the situation or not. Probably no one else but him was able to understand it. Maybe it was a habit. I was accepted for engineering at university two years ago, and he was not. He had no choice other than going to mandatory military service. And now he was back from the military service, thankfully not harmed bodily. But I could sometimes see the signs of depression or anger in his behavior, compared to the time of high school when he was quite a playful boy.

He fell in love with a beautiful girl. A love which could result in nothing but more pain to his distracted mind after military service. The girl's family was very strict in following the traditions and were expecting a wealthy man to marry their daughter, while our society was troubled by a religious revolution.

He was very talented in my opinion, but he was not satisfied to do a regular program in university. Sometimes he was astonishingly smart. But he was looking for something perfect. That's why I often told him, "If you get married, you might ruin both lives - yours and your wife's." We were hanging out in the late summer.

"I recommend you start a university program as soon as you can. That helps you a lot. You are talented and you should not waste your time," I encouraged him.

"University helping me...Seriously...like how it has helped you." Then he mocked me: "University will help you". And continued, "Has it helped you at all? Who will you be after spending your life penniless in a school? Einstein?"

I tried to explain that although university is not a way to gain fast and easy money, it is the best way for a talented youth like him to grow his creativity and establish a strong lifestyle for himself and become helpful to others. And at the end I said, "If you are not satisfied with the Iranian universities, then you need to go to another country…what you need is a new place…a new place that welcomes your talents."

With my words he jolted aggressively and said, "You don't know anything about the reality of our world. Money only talks to other money. Power talks to other power. They don't care about me and you or other people like me and you. I want to be rich, then I can be powerful."

"How?" I asked.

"Do you know all the days that you have spent staggered after the so-called "Cultural Revolution" waiting to go back to school, how much money some people have gained from the fluctuation of currency exchange in the black market?"

"What do you mean? I don't know about the black market of currency exchange or any other black market because I don't like dirty businesses."

"That's why I said you don't know nothing… OK…tell me, how many days does a year have? Now let's assume that there is no leap year at all, and all years are the same 365 days. OK? Now tell me, do you know how many circulars in the past 365 days have been issued by the central bank of Iran and many other departments to dictate how many US dollars this or that person can buy and what is the exchange rate and many things like that?"

"So, again so what?" I replied indifferently.

"No, I know what I must do. I don't waste my time. I don't waste my life. I have seen how easily I can play a role in this scrambled market. I can take my share of money and my share of happiness."

"Your share? Are you talking about happiness on the black market? Don't you know it's a sort of theft?"

"No. It's not theft at all. I follow all circulars issued by the central bank. I just know how to talk to whom. No theft at all. I just know how to make the senior managers happy. That's it."

17

"Then you are obliged to them. You must do what they want. It could move you to many strange situations. You might be involved with something unjust. It could be life threatening. Seriously, life threatening to you and to others."

To avoid more arguments, we started walking in the street until we reached an old pastry shop that had been in our hometown for generations. The smell of sugar, cream and vanilla was very seductive, and changed our mood. I invited my friend to eat some pastry. Young people can usually change their moods with delicious food or drink, something that would be a dream at an older age.

We entered the pastry shop. An old-style building with a row of glass fridges in front of the shop. The familiar, elderly owner of the shop was working alone that day. He welcomed us. The wonderful smell of pastries with the cool air of the shop was charming. I offered to buy two pieces of cake with cream and colorful jelly mixed with cherries. Instead, my friend pointed to something at the other end of shop and murmured something that I could not understand. The old owner moved slowly toward the end of shop, and I followed him with my eyes. When I turned to my friend to ask him what exactly he had asked for, I saw him in the walkway gesturing at me as if he wanted me to come out of the pastry shop. Then he moved his hand urgently and shouted, "Come out, we don't need anything." I apologized politely and came out to follow my friend who was laughing and running backward while still looking at me. Then he opened his hand with two pieces of pie in it. He gave one piece to me with a loud laugh and started to bite another one.

"Did you steal it?" I screamed. "Are we not able to buy it? How many kilos do you want?"

My reaction and facial expression were probably shocking. I was not able to control my anger. My friend's smile froze on his face, and I threw the pie in the garbage bin at the side of walkway. We hurried to the other side of the street toward a long stairway that was the connection between this street to another one at a lower elevation. I hurried down without knowing why. The smell of sugar, cream and vanilla on my hand was disgusting. I was trying to clean my hands when I saw a man who was distributing pamphlets for preparatory classes for the university exam. I took a pamphlet and angrily cleaned my hands with it. I mumbled, "What has he gained from military service?"

At the end of the stairs close to a bus station I stood and turned my head to watch my friend who was coming lazily down the stairs to join me. He looked hollow, and sad. To avoid eye contact with him, I looked around. In the bus station a young mother was struggling to control her two little boys while she had to look after her heavy grocery bags too. She was in a dark rough dress and scarf on that hot summer afternoon. The overwhelmed mom was holding the hands of her playful little boys, trying hard to keep them close to her. The boys were fighting, running back and forth, giggling, mocking each other, and spinning around their mom. Their mom had held the hand of each boy tightly, nervously watching for the bus's arrival, and looking after her grocery bags, while her boys had pulled her arms in opposite directions as if she was crucified.

In the late afternoon of that very day, we heard that a war had been started between our country and the other one. A neighbouring country had attacked Iran.

EMPTY BOXES

Today, after a daily wandering, I was rummaging for my running shoes in the closet and my luggage, but I found a book instead. Although it was long forgotten, strangely it was still with me after many years and even during my travel to Greece. The book was a play entitled "Who's Afraid of Virginia Woolf?" by Edward Albee which we were supposed to read for our art class.

This book reminded me of one of my classmates who was nicknamed Cengiz Khan by us, his classmates. We used to call him Cengiz Khan because he was strong, brave, and very clever. I still can remember the day he argued seriously to convince our Algebra teacher about the correct answer to a question. He was good at reading books and writing some poetry and literary essays. He wrote an essay about "Who's Afraid of Virginia Woolf?". Cengiz Khan also brought us this idea that we should play this play in our school.

A group of students including me and Cengiz Khan spoke to our art teacher and convinced him to let us start reading this play and practice it after school in one of the classrooms. We bought three copies of this book and started. After a few days of our group reading, the principal of our school called us to the office and told us that we should stop the group reading and practicing the play. Apparently, our principal was terrified, because in those days after the Iranian Revolution in 1979, such gatherings of a group of students, especially for reading a book like "Who's Afraid of Virginia Woolf?" was ringing an alarm about the possibility of political activity. And it was known that the Revolutionary government had an aggressive attitude towards all political activities that were out of its very restricted circle. Thus, we were obliged to stop our group reading and practicing "Who's Afraid of Virginia Woolf'?" in school or even somewhere else out of the school. So, for that reason, we were forbidden to continue our work to put on the play. It would have been difficult anyway because we did not have any student girl in our school to act with us. In fact, all schools including ours had been gender segregated. It is a very inflexible rule, even now. Each school could be either for girls or for boys and no one of one gender is allowed to enter a school meant for the other.

The day we were all desperately stopped in our group reading, Cengiz Khan and I had a short conversation on our way home.

"Why reading a book should be problematic?" Cengiz Khan said.

"They might consider it as a political action, and I have heard of some youth that are arrested for gatherings like this. The Revolutionary Guard even controls the books. Some books are forbidden. Some bookstores are shut down and I have even seen one of them that was burned by hardliners." I replied.

"So, what youth should do?"

"I really don't know. It's very nasty…frustrating."

"No… it is not only frustrating…it's gross…it's dangerous. It's life threatening…"

"So…what are we supposed to do? The Revolutionary Guard and government consider everything as a threat to their reign."

"All what I know – and I'm sure about it – is that I am a human being. A young human. I need to learn. I need to live freely. I need to be active. I need to be productive. I am not dangerous per se. Not letting me grow freely is a real danger, it's a real threat to myself, you, everyone, and a threat to the country too. Why don't they understand it?"

We spent a few moments in silence. Then Cengiz Khan continued, "A new place…a new place that's what everyone like me need to grow. A new place helps me to grow…not a place that limits my abilities without any real reason…a place that I can ask "why" for any situation…and have right to choose my direction…all I need is a new place…a place to grow. Living under suppression is life threatening…believe me."

A few years later in an early summer evening, I met my high school art teacher who had initially allowed us to practice "Who's Afraid of Virginia Woolf?", retired, gray and stressed. He was disposing of some empty boxes outside of his house. "May I help you?" I asked him. "Help?" he sardonically smiled. "You cannot fill up the empty boxes, I guess." He stopped moving the empty boxes and straightened his back with a short sigh and frown, as if it was a painful movement for him. "Now, people want to visit my gallery if there is any" he said with another sardonic smile. He continued, "All these past years I worked hard, but there is nothing left to present as the results." Then he laughed...

My cellphone rings and wakes me from the daydreams that were triggered by "Who's Afraid of Virginia Woolf?". A friend who had known Cengiz Khan too was on the other side of the call, from a far city in Iran. He said, "Cengiz Khan died."

That was very shocking news to me, and the voice of my friend was expressing his huge sadness too.

"Why? How?"

"I don't know. People say that he committed suicide. But I think he had a heart attack because of drug abuse."

"He was drug addicted? That seems unlikely to me. Like other friends, I was positive, too, that he will become a good engineer, or a mathematician."

"Didn't he tell you that his application to the university was refused? He was once arrested because of participating in a political demonstration."

"No, I haven't seen him for many years."

"Sometimes we had met each other. I helped him to find a job. In a telecommunication station. It was far away from the city. He used to work as an operator of a microwave relay system. The job was a tough one. You know how being close to the microwave antenna affects the nerves. He had to stay at the station, far from his home, for at least two weeks, and had only one week's rest after every two weeks staying at the station. His wife couldn't stand that and divorced."

"He was married?"

"Yes, and had a little daughter too. The last time I met him was about six months ago. He told me what if he was able to immigrate to another country. If that happens, then probably, he can convince his ex-wife to come with him, and with his daughter. He loved his daughter too much."

"Then, what did he do for immigration?"

"I don't know. Perhaps nothing. Anyway, he didn't have any savings. I was thinking if you can help him to immigrate."

"Help? What help am I supposed to do?"

"Now? Nothing."

A CRUMPLED WRAPPING PAPER

It was returned almost one month later with the words "MOVED – RETURN TO SENDER" written on the box. This was when the European Union was founded in the early 90s.

One day, I unexpectedly met one of my university classmates again. He was a few years older than me, a soccer player, a tall and strong young man who was an attractive character for all the single girls at the university. But he got married while we were still classmates, and he was only twenty-one years old. I used to call him "Gone with the Hormones" to make fun of him by mocking the name of that famous movie *Gone with the Wind**. In return he called me "Bookworm." That was true, I was always reading books, especially poetry, in my spare time. I was able to recite an intriguing verse for any situation. Such poems that everyone nodded in response, although I was not exactly sure what that nodding meant.

I had not seen my old classmate for many years. He had been working for an aviation company. We met each other in an airport on the way back from one of his business trips to Europe. He looked older than his age, with some gray hair, wrinkles on his face and a little fat belly. He had got divorced, and he had two daughters, one teenager and another one three or four years younger. That unexpected meeting excited us and made us happy. But he seemed more excited, and I thought that he was looking for someone to talk to. He gave me his phone number and address.

We met again a few days later in his apartment. Everything was covered with dust. Shoes, shirts, plates, and other things were scattered here and there. Apparently, his daughters were living with their mother most of the time. The place was so cluttered that there was nowhere to sit and talk other than the balcony.

---

*   "Gone with the Wind" is a 1939 American movie directed by Victor Fleming.

I cannot collect my mind and stay for a long time in a messy place. We grabbed two chairs and sat on the balcony, and he talked about his divorce and then about his recent trip to Europe. He said that after his divorce he decided to live alone forever, but on his trip, he met a lady in Berlin who made him change his mind and how he saw the world. He talked differently, much differently than how he used to talk when we were classmates. Now he was all romantic and drowning with such feeling that he had met his dream woman. He had fallen in love with a lady who was working in the company of their vendor. He was surprised when I tried to talk to him logically. I told him that his dream might not necessarily come true.

"Is that all you've learned from the poetry that you are proud of?" he asked sarcastically.

"What about your daughters?" I asked.

"They are living with their mom, right? And I pay them half of my salary every month, right?" He replied.

We spoke that night and some other nights together. He was starving for long, intimate conversations. I was his only friend who was still single, had some free time and some poetic sense. But there were times that he was very silent. When he was puffing on his cigarette and staring at nowhere. I was not sure what he was seeing at those moments, but I could imagine that he was strolling in the lovely moments of his trip to Berlin.

He was eager to do something for his new love. One day he called me for another talk. When I met him, I was surprised to see him very determined to buy a precious gift and send it to that lady. We talked about different gifts. He didn't like the idea of sending something like a carpet or perfume. He said sardonically, "Am I going to send her an advertising thing? Such things look like an advertising key chain or wall calendar." He was thinking that certain items such as those could be thought of as business gifts, mere advertising for a company. He was looking for something authentic that could show his deep and sincere love. While he was talking, I could see that his wrinkles had become deeper, and his hair grayer. I thought to myself, what is he looking for in this love?

The last suggestion which he accepted was to buy a special book. I knew a publisher who specialized in publishing very old poetry books, books that had been illustrated by masters of miniature centuries ago. The kind of books that had been kept for centuries in the library of kings and were now in glass boxes in museums. The publisher used to provide a limited number of high-quality prints of such books with an English translation of some pages and a fancy box for the book too. This suggestion made my old classmate very excited, and he decided to buy a book and send it with a letter to his love as soon as possible. Of course, I didn't say that the publisher probably had counted on selling these books to some very rich companies, hoping they might buy these fancy books to give to their special and wealthy customers as an advertising gift.

When we were wrapping the book and letter before posting it, I suggested that we fill the box with some scrap paper so that the book and letter would remain safe during transportation. He seemed disgusted by this idea. He fancied his gift and his letter being very nicely presented. He was hoping to present his gift to his love as delicately as the verses and miniatures within the book.

Now it had been returned. The box had been damaged and had become a little wet in the transportation. We sat again on the balcony. That evening, he was smoking a cigarette and asked me to read some poetry. I tried to joke instead, but he seemed serious. I recited something like "Passing time is a pregnant lady that delivers a child named forgetfulness." At the end I added, "Time reconciles everything and will help us to forget." He replied immediately, "Or will help us to die." I was shocked. Is he thinking of suicide? I decided not to leave and stayed with him that night.

The next day at my work, I must have seemed tired and overwhelmed, because one of my colleagues asked me, "Are you sick?" I explained to him about the divorce of my old classmate but said nothing about his new love and the book. Then I continued, "I am worried about him".

My colleague listened to me and then said, "The best solution is to introduce a decent woman to him."

Those days in Iran, girls, and boys —or men and women— did not have many opportunities to talk together or become acquainted before marriage. Introducing girls and boys for arranged marriages was something desirable for many people, although young people did not like that because they saw love and arranged marriages as contradictory.

"Introducing?" I asked, "Two persons who know nothing about each other?"

"Listen," said my colleague, "it will be all right. I am telling you. You know your friend and I know the lady who is working in the registry of our company. They will become acquainted if you and I help them. You should help your friend," he insisted.

My colleague had been married about two years ago and his son was two or three months old. He told me that the lady who was working in the registry of our company was divorced before she was hired. She had been married for about ten years and her son, her only child, had died a few years after her wedding. Her son had been diagnosed with Thalassemia in the first year of his life. She and her husband had tried everything that could be bought by money, but unfortunately their son died. The loss devastated both wife and husband and made them sick. Apparently, her husband started to smoke opium. The smoker husband made his wife frustrated and their cracked life ended with divorce. Then my colleague proudly continued, "I helped her to get hired by the company, and now she has recovered a lot." In a philosophical way he said, "Two injured hearts understand each other better." He tried to reassure me that "my old classmate" and "the lady of the registry" could recover together faster and more easily.

"What about his daughters?" I asked, "Do you know he has two daughters?"

"Even better," said my colleague. "She has lost her son. Do you know how she will feel as a mother for the daughters of your friend?"

Although I was not so naive to accept the story of opium that had always been a good cover-up for other private problems as a reason for divorce, I could not simply believe that two injured hearts could understand each other through a simple introduction. But I had no experience of having a child or any true feeling as a parent, and I was thinking of two young girls and a mother who had lost her son. Also, I was thinking about a potential solution for both groups. Thinking of a good and happy ending was what convinced me. It seemed the only practical way to help my old classmate, especially in a society where relationships were restricted.

But it did not happen easily, and my old classmate was not an easy man, especially in that situation. However, after several afternoon conversations with him while we were seated on the balcony, my old classmate eventually accepted my colleague's invitation to a tea and poetry gathering. Such short and simple meetings continued between the three of us, my old classmate, my colleague, and myself. We met several afternoons in the house of my colleague or in a café to spend some time having philosophical debates, jokes, and discussions while we drank tea. My colleague was humorous and knew how to make enticing events that would attract the attendee to another similar tea party. After a few such gatherings, my old classmate and I were invited to a dinner party at my colleague's house. My colleague insisted that I should help my old classmate get prepared for the event.

That afternoon, I went to my old classmate's apartment first, and helped him choose a beautiful suit and tie. Again, we wrapped that special book in beautiful wrapping papers, because my old classmate was convinced to bring it as a gift to that dinner party, although we did not talk about to whom that gift should be given. I also asked my old classmate to bring his daughters with him to the dinner party too. "It's good for all of you." I just repeated the sentence that I had heard from my colleague. Then I went home to review some poetry books and get prepared for a "Cinderella event."

After an hour, I walked toward my colleague's house. I was the first guest. My colleague and his wife were busy with many preparations. Although his wife was occupied with many

28

necessary things that she had to do for her baby, she had been able to set the table beautifully with pastry and tea. The aroma of some wonderful food came from the kitchen. The second guest was the lady from the registry. When she entered with a beautiful bouquet, I realized how uncivilized I was because I had come empty handed. After exchanging the usual pleasantries, the two ladies sat together to talk and then the lady from the registry went to help our host with the preparation of dinner. My colleague and I started rummaging for music CDs and were arguing about which one to play.

Lastly my old classmate and his two daughters joined us. I was unsure about what had happened. My old classmate was not wearing a tie and seemed distraught. I did not know what had happened when he had picked up his daughters, but I knew that his daughters were living with their mom in another house, which was probably their grandparents' house.

He had brought that special book that we had wrapped together for the second time. He did not give it to anyone and when he sat down, he put it on another chair close to the balcony.

His daughters were pale and uncomfortable. The older girl looked angry, while the younger girl was agitated. The younger was carrying her school bag, presumably for doing her homework. I could understand her feelings. I thought that she had been forced to bring her school bag to a dinner party. When I was a schoolboy, I hated taking my homework to parties.

With the arrival of my old classmate, we were three men arguing and laughing about selecting the most interesting CD and which one should be played first.

On the other side of the room, I saw the two ladies trying hard to welcome the girls. A great show of kindness that was disturbing to the sisters. Apparently, they did not feel comfortable with that exaggerated kindness.

The two sisters unintentionally were trying to keep themselves close to the corner of the room. I imagined these two girls were acting like two little chickens that were stuck to the corner of a cage assuming the walls could protect them.

Although these two sisters were uncomfortable at that party, they were also fighting silently with each other. The older girl whispered to the younger and the younger replied to her sister. Whispers and frowns were being exchanged in their hidden fighting. Meanwhile, the wife of my colleague left the room to look after her baby in the other room and the lady from the registry tried to get closer to the girls and talk to them. Normally, the first option for starting a conversation in such circumstances would be looking at the notebooks and books and saying, "Wow, what a beautiful book, how smart you are," but this attempt evidently seemed meaningless to both sides. After about half an hour, the lady from the registry felt that she was not successful in her attempt.

The absence of my colleague's wife took a long time, so my colleague went to help his wife. After a few minutes both returned with their crying baby in the mother's arms. At least the baby was a reason for changing the atmosphere. The lady from the registry left the girls to look at the chubby baby. Again, some pleasant words like, "Wow, what a beautiful boy," and smiles were exchanged. The ladies were either busy with the chubby baby or with preparing food in the kitchen while the sisters continued their silent fight.

My old classmate felt he had nothing better to do but to go to the balcony and I thought he went to smoke a cigarette. My colleague whispered in my ear, "Why did he bring his daughters? "Because you said so," I replied perplexed. "You said she will be happy to be their mom."

My colleague looked at me with impatience. "Let's start with some music and jokes and inviting the girls to dance," my colleague said.

"That will change the air," I replied and started telling jokes, laughing, and asking for help to find a good CD. But my attempt was met with no response because the two young girls were still agitated with their silent fighting.

Suddenly the younger girl started crying, but not loudly. The older daughter hurried to the washroom saying that she had a stomachache. My colleague's wife and the lady from the registry exchanged a meaningful glance and my colleague's wife whispered something to her friend which I only heard a part of "...pain of puberty..." My colleague tried to talk to the younger girl to make her calm. The lady from the registry said that her migraine had just returned. Once the older girl came out of the washroom, the lady from the registry went to the washroom to take her migraine pill.

My old classmate came back from the balcony and whispered to his daughters. "Well, we will go back home...Get ready."

When he was saying, "We will leave..." the lady from the registry came out of washroom. I saw that she had washed her make up off completely, and her scarf was tightened over her hair like when she worked in the company. Pale and agitated, the lady from the registry took her purse to show her readiness to leave. When both groups were ready to leave, my colleague said to my old classmate, "Well, it's too early...however...I think you can drive Miss—(the lady from the registry) home." By saying this he was hoping my old classmate would drive her to her home to get them better acquainted. But my old classmate apologized and said that he would be taking a taxi and added, "Oh, it seems I have left my lighter on the balcony" and he rushed to the balcony.

When he came back from the balcony, my old classmate whispered into my ear "I'll take a taxi, just return my car... Don't say anything to anybody...the car key is on the balcony...Don't say anything..."

In my old classmate's last words and actions while he was leading his daughters from the apartment, I could see he had returned to his original character. In those moments he seemed like a soccer player, though older with a weaker body and nerves.

With this undesirable ending, our gathering scattered like when people leave a movie theatre. I confess that I was nervous too and was looking for a proper time and an acceptable excuse to go to the balcony to get the car key. I pretended that I was helping my hosts arrange the chairs. My colleague and his wife were taking plates, cups, and dishes back to the kitchen. They were not talking together in front of me, but when they were in the kitchen, I could hear his wife saying to my colleague "...love or...pity?"

I rushed to the balcony to get the car key. I found it and I also saw that special book. The special book that my old classmate and I had wrapped up that afternoon was now left on the balcony. The beautiful wrapping paper had been torn off, crumpled, and tossed as a piece of garbage in the corner of the balcony. The car key had been left there on the box of that special book beside some cigarette butts on that dark silent balcony.

II
THERE

AN AFFORDABLE LOVE

How many days have passed since our last meeting? I'm still waiting for that moment that will turn all sadness and worries into hope and joy.

"If you don't brew the tea well, its taste makes you even more sad and angry," said the old lady who sat next to us on the bus. She said that she was always telling her daughter this, because she kept getting new bottles of pills from the pharmacy because of her headaches.

We were passing the Bosphorus Bridge that connects the Asian part of Istanbul to its European part. You remember Sultan Ahmed's Mosque and bazaar? Was it called the Blue Mosque? Why are most of the mosques located in the Asian part of the city when the Ottoman's castle is in the European part?

The old lady who sat next to us said she had searched every corner of the Bazaar to find a good tea. You whispered to me, "She said so to express her terrible headache." We were passing the middle of the bridge when you found a migraine pill in your purse. The old lady then became surprised and happy when she accepted the pill from you. She swallowed the pill with a gulp of water from her water bottle.

You said Türkiye is a terrible place for refugees. You were determined to meet with a young lady that you had heard of. You didn't know her. All you knew was that she had applied for asylum at the UN office in Türkiye because of her homosexuality. You didn't promote her homosexuality as the reason for your interest in meeting with her, but I didn't see any other reason for your sudden decision, although I didn't tell you.

"Türkiye? It's a Muslim country too. How could she survive here?" I said. You replied, "The issue is not the religion that the government represents. We all, regardless of our religion, are generally against free living and self-expression. That's the problem."

I could not agree with you leaving me again to find an unknown lady. I could not imagine any responsibility for either of us to help others while we ourselves were unstable yet.

The hotel only used teabags to brew tea. We both were angry then. You said that you wanted to travel from Istanbul to Van, a city in the other side of Türkiye close to the border of Iran, to meet that unknown young lady.

We had just started our journey from the orange gardens in Shiraz toward the bluest sea in Europe after almost one year of struggling together about how to make our final decision. We had decided to immigrate first, then marry. It seemed strange to many people around us. You were always saying that "marriage is a bigger immigration, I believe." And that was the reason why we did not marry when we were living in Shiraz before our immigration.

I had known you from the university. You knew me too. One day you told me, "You were not the best student boy, and I was not the most beautiful student girl." However, I convinced you that I love you and we should marry happily. After I finished my studies. I started working for a manufacturing company, and two years later you started working in a hospital. Although you did not like your job. You liked to spend most of your time strolling in the fig or orange gardens outside of the city. One day you said working with the human body is disgusting.

The night before we were supposed to leave Istanbul for Larnaka in Cyprus, you decided to return to Van instead. "Are you serious? Do you want to go all the way back to the other side of Türkiye?" I reminded you of the troubles we had faced so far to reach to this situation and why we must appreciate it as our first step, but you did not listen to me. I even fought with you as you were leaving the hotel for the train station. I shouted, "It's a terrible idea! Why are you going back? To seek what? Love? Humanity? The only thing that you have gained from working in the hospital is taking migraine pills. Only migraine pills… why?"

And you shouted back, "Didn't you know the horizon escapes farther from you while you're trying to get closer? Didn't anyone tell you the horizon is in your eyes? Mine…ours? Didn't anyone tell you the poisoner is our own taste? No one can defeat it. It flows in my blood, to my every single nerve and cell. Didn't you know love is the cruelest thing?"

Then I had nothing to do but going to the northern part of Cyprus that is under control of Türkiye. I passed the gate which is in the middle of barbed wires and traveled to Larnaka by bus, alone. I traveled on the bus of a group of tourists. In this trip I heard from the bus driver who said, "All the historical places around the world that attract you were built only because of a bloody war". He was a middle-aged man, who had memories from the war that had happened in 1974. But he was an active and happy driver too. He told jokes and sang some songs for his passengers during our trip.

I was counting the brutal wars that had been happened in the modern era while I was passing the door between the Turkish part and the independent part of Cyprus, and while I was in the bus. Cyprus looked to me the crossing point of Asia, Africa, and Europe. I passed the partition of Cyprus enshrouded by the barbed wire of UN-monitored Green Line. I was heading to Larnaca, a city on the southern coast of Cyprus for a few days rest on a Mediterranean beach and search for a way to go to Greece. I was dreaming of leaving myself in the sunlight and watching a schooner in a lovely breeze.

We arrived, discharged into a hotel located in a busy street at night, with hotels, bars, and restaurants. It was a hot day; I sat in the lobby of the hotel after a long boring trip. It was almost evening, and the street was getting busier and busier. One or two tours arrived from Tehran, and one or two were about to leave the hotel. A group of girls graduated BSc. or MSc. that had been accepted for PhD. from Princeton or Caltech were checking the address of the American Embassy for obtaining their visas. They were talking with a group of similar girls that were leaving that hotel and had already obtained them.

An elderly woman originally from Cyprus with fluent in English was seated beside me, napping on the couch of lobby. She started talking to me politely, blaming the people that were talking too loudly because they were disturbing her comfort. I shared my empathy with her and expressed my tiredness too. I said that I had traveled by bus from Nicosia, and I also addressed the barbed wire of UN-monitored Green Line. That made her start whimpering and talking about the history of that war and how she and some other people had been deprived after that invasion. And that is why she is living in that hotel, although the government is paying for the cost, and she wouldn't be disrespectful, but the hotel had become very uncomfortable because the government had allowed many tourists to come to her city. I was nodding my understanding for her although since I was a tourist, I was also trying to explain that tourism is a good source of income and so and so… but simultaneously my other ear was involved in hearing another conversation.

The tour leader of one of the tours that were leaving the hotel toward Tehran was talking with a young man who was probably a student or a temporary worker in Larnaka.

Apparently, the young man was begging the tour leader to give his letter to his mother in Tehran. I stole a glance; tears were circled in his eyes. The young man was whining that it's expensive to send his mother a bouquet or have a trip to visit her or invite her to Cyprus. And he continued that he had not taken any trip after he arrived in Cyprus many years ago. The envelope he gave to the tour leader was illustrated with a picture of some beautiful coral bells. The tour leader hastily took the letter and assured the young man that he will deliver it in a day after his arrival.

Then the tour leader turned toward a young lady who came with two cups of coffee in her hands. The tour leader took one of the cups with lovely appreciation. Then they hugged each other passionately and kissed each other several times.

Apparently, the young lady was living in Larnaka because she said to him, "and again you are leaving."

"I have to leave…how else could I come back again?" the tour leader said and laughed, expecting a happy laugh from the young lady. The young lady didn't laugh, but said, "Coming back after three or four months…Yes?"

"That's my job…don't you know how busy I am?"

"Busy? Can't you start a business here? Easier…safer…and happier?"

The tour leader spent a few moments in silence. He tried to collect his thoughts, and change his mood from a playful lovely man to a reasonable and logical character, "Well…it's not as easy as you think…don't you know how difficult it was to hire you in this travel agency? You should be very thankful for that."

"Thankful? Yes, I am, but I'll be more thankful if you stay here as you have promised at the beginning."

"Should I stay here? Who should work and make money then? Will you stay with me without money?"

The hands of the young lady started to shake nervously. She blushed. Then she said with a trembling voice, "You do have enough money… You can start a business here if you want…but you don't want to stay here more than one or two weeks every three or four months." Then her tears flowed.

"Why are you crying? It's not good in the moment of departure…so why don't you come to Tehran to live together with me?"

"I cannot. You know that I cannot come back to Tehran. And I don't believe you spend all your time in Tehran too. You travel with other tours to other places most of your time. I'm crying because you said I want you because of your money. You know I've handled my life very well before meeting you. But if it's as you said, and I want you for your money, then what do you expect of me…" then she ran out of the lobby while she was sobbing heavily.

I felt nervous after what I heard from the tour leader and the young lady. I turned back to the old lady who was seated beside me and was still talking about the history of war and tourists. I asked her, "Where could I find a well brewed tea?" She pointed to the other side of the lobby and said, "On that counter, they might sell tea bags and boiled water."

BLOGGER

When I came to Dubai, we played video games together. Yes, I hesitated. But you laughed happily and forced me to pick a character to play.

After the game was over, I told you, "I loved drawing cartoons on the white border of my textbooks. One frame on each page. The pictures were very simple. I used to draw a stick man made of a circle as his head and a line as his trunk, two lines for the arms and two lines for the legs. One frame of his movement on each page. The characters in these video games remind me of that stick man. When I grabbed all the pages of book between my thumb and the rest of my fingers and allowed the pages of the book overlap one by one, the stick man was moving. He was running seriously and determinedly. As if he was escaping from something. Or trying to gain something, earnestly. After he had been running and running, suddenly an obstacle would appear in front of him. I had drawn that barrier. The stick man would have to jump over the obstacle and continue his hard work to reach the next one. That had been drawn by me too. The stick man never seemed tired and never gave up running. Watching his serious tries had been enjoyable. It even started to seem to me that he would feel discouraged if there was nothing in his way. It was like there was a contract between us. I would put new obstacles in his path, he was responsible to jump over each one precisely and on time."

I had come to Dubai to do the IELTS exam that I needed for immigration. At that time, due to some political reasons, the IELTS exam was not being held in Tehran. So, I came to Dubai to do my exam.

After the writing-exam of IELTS, as you can imagine how important it was to me, I was very tired. I came out of the exam place to walk around the educational complex that the IELTS examination center was in the middle of. I needed to refresh my mind and was interested to see how students like you were entertaining themselves there. Some students, which I guess most of them were Iranian, had been mingling, talking together, and laughing in the hallways or in the cafeteria hall.

When I stepped to a wide-open area with benches and trees, I met a middle-aged man like your father. I mean, if we assumed – just assumed – he was your father, it would not be a wrong assumption. Well, that man had seemed a wealthy person. Of course, not a very top rich person, but rich enough to be able to invest in the education of his children. I am sorry to say that, but he was very overwhelmed, and sad, with an insecure feeling for himself and his daughter's future.

Once we met and he realized that we both could talk in Persian language, he invited me to sit beside him on a bench. He explained that he had purchased an apartment for his daughter in Dubai around 2007, considering that it would be a good opportunity for his daughter to live and study here untroubled. And certainly, he had counted on the appreciation of his apartment's value too. But now, after the recession of 2008, he was seeing that all his hopes were melting down. He had a feeling of helplessness. And he was very concerned about his daughter. I imagined he had many private concerns about his daughter that he was not comfortable talking about to me. But he said that his wife always tells their friends and families that her daughter will graduate as a medical doctor soon. Then he puffed on his cigarette very deeply, and tears circled in his eyes.

Yes, your father – as we assumed he was your father – had been desperately concerned and overwhelmed while he was watching his fortune melt down and his hopes for his daughter disappear. At that moment he needed only a person for an intimate talk. Only a short but intimate talk.

You invited me to play video games again. You are obsessed with new technology. Well, I am too, but probably not as much as you are. I said, "I like books on paper and classic movies". That made you laugh and mock me again. Anyway, I played some video games with you. And watched how you win every time.

41

But I am not sure I have seen what you have seen in those animation characters. The video games seemed boring to me. I tried to talk about that distressed man and remind you of your parents' expectations, instead.

You asked me with your normal tone, but apparently a little frustrated, "What do my parents need to be satisfied? Why are they so worried?"

"They need to see your future is guaranteed."

"My future? OK...They want to see my warranty certificate? Like a manufacturer's certificate when we buy a TV...Right? Then you giggled, distracted. "I'm not a TV, nor a vacuum cleaner, nor a slow cooker."

I tried to not show my frustration, so I said slowly, drawing my words out as if I was practicing the words for the IELTS exam, "No one has said you are a TV or something like that. Your parents want you obtain a good education, a secure job with a good income, and a happy marriage."

You then played a ballerina character in response. You were still trying to hide your frustration. You raised your arms and head toward the sky, walked tiptoed delicately, and then as if you are reciting some holy verses, repeated slowly with a sad tone, "Oh, good educations... oh, good fortunes...oh, happy marriages...embrace me."

I was seated on the sofa, looking down, thinking how I could express my right feelings to you and how could I understand you correctly. You sat on the carpet in front of me and looked directly into my eyes and asked, "Can you, or my parents point to a successful example? Can someone show me a person in my age or a little older happy with his or her education, income, and marriage?"

I only remained silent. Then you turned on the TV and started searching for various music channels. I had known that you like modern music too, and you listen most to American songs, and some of the Persian songs, especially from the Persian singers who lived in Los Angles.

You chose an English song. You took your comb as a fake microphone. You started lip reading that song and dancing with it very seriously. You danced very energetically, as if you were doing that in front of audiences. When the song finished you asked me, "Didn't you like it?"

"Why not? You danced all the time. And you looked so happy. You tore up all your papers and threw them in the air. You were very happy and satisfied. You danced with your own shadow all that time."

"My shadow? Why didn't you join me in dancing?"

I remained silent because I didn't want to say something confusing. Also, at the same time I was thinking about the proper questions that I could ask you to understand you better.

You put your comb in your drawer, and then you cat-walked to pick up my socks that were on the carpet near my shoes in front of your apartment entrance. You wore them as a pair of gloves. Each sock was a puppet now. Then you hid yourself behind your armchair. You raised your hands from the sides of armchair. You changed your voice to the voice of a sentimental girl for your right hand and to an arrogant young man for your left hand. And you were moving your fingers to express the actions and conversations between these two puppets.

The girl: "Oh, where are you my beloved prince?"

The man: "Oh, my love…my love…I'm on my way."

The girl: "Oh, come and take me to the dreamland."

The man: "I love you…I love you."

The girl: "I love you more…"

The man: "It's the time for us to get married…I will destroy all obstacles in our way toward happiness."

The girl: "And I will be with you all the time. I will be your courage…and I will be your reward after all your battles."

The man: "Oh, I love you with all my cells."

The girl: "Oh, I love you with all my nerves."

Then the puppets moved romantically toward each other. They hugged each other very passionately. They kissed each other several times. Then after a few seconds that the puppets remained clutched together, they separated from each other slowly and hesitantly.

The girl, with a nasal voice as if she talks with a stuffed nose to protect herself from a bad smell, "Eww!...you smell gross."

The man, with the same reaction as if he wants to protect himself from a bad smell too, "What? I smell gross! No...it's you who spread a gross smell around...not me."

The girl: "No. You smell gross."

The man: You smell gross...you."

Then you clenched your fingers and the puppets started hitting and scolding each other. They continued hitting each other badly until each fell on one side of the armchair.

Then you picked up each sock with one of your hands and carried them between your thumb and your forefinger. You cat-walked toward me. You swung those smelly socks in front of my face like two pendulums and said, "Happy ending...don't you like it?"

The socks smelled gross. I snatched them from your hands and threw them close to the entrance of your apartment. And I smiled reluctantly. You sat in front of me. We both spent a few seconds in silence. Then you spoke with your normal voice, "I know some of my friends. Close to my age or a few years older. My parents know them too. You might know them as well. Or probably you know some of your friends with the same condition. Many of them have a good education. Some have good jobs and good incomes. Most of them are married a few years ago then divorced. Some have a little child too. Those who have continued their married life are not happy. And those who are divorced have even more troubles. Because of their family or because of society. The friends I am talking about sometimes come to Dubai, or travel to other places for their vacation or something like that. They come here to remove their scarf from their heads. To use cosmetics. To buy and wear brands. They eat fast food in the food court. But still, they are not happy. I assure you. I know them, and I talk to them very often. A few weeks ago, a friend of mine who is a physician was here. In fact, I invited her to come. I bought a concert ticket for her too. Do you know why? Because she was very depressed. A young physician. With a good income, but she is divorced. And she has a baby. When I realized how stressed she is I convinced her to leave her little daughter with her mother and come here for a little relaxation. You know what happened? She didn't enjoy her trip at all, and I got stressed too. Her thoughts were always with her little daughter."

"I understand it. It is like what your parents feel about you. Like what I feel. Now, suppose you forgot me. At least talk to your parents about your future. What's on your mind? What do you want to be?"

"A blogger."

"What? How can you make your living by spending your time writing a blog?

"I am a blogger. Come and see my blog."

You pulled my hand to come with you by your computer desk. You opened your blog and we looked at some of your posts. The most impressive one was a photo of a young boy who had been carrying a huge bag of garbage on his back. He looked desperately at the camera. The description you had written about this photo was very short, "In Tehran. In 21st century."

I was totally perplexed. I had no idea about the future of being a blogger. Also, I felt that I was not able to reject your opinions. In fact, your ideas were correct in many areas. Then I said, "OK, do that, but don't lose your youth. Time flies fast as you know."

"But I don't harm anybody," you said.

And I replied with a low voice, "Love is not harmful in my opinion."

You didn't answer me. And we spent a few moments in silence. Then I told you, "Let's watch something that shows liveliness, like a thoughtful love." You laughed at me then. You grumbled and threw the TV remote at me and said, "Very well, now it's your turn... find something for us to watch..." And you giggled again as always.

I searched for Casablanca*. "What is Casablanca?" you asked me. And I explained the role of North Africa in WWII. I said, "Many cities are founded on lust and fortune, as history shows." I continued, "Gambling which is an attempt to gain a quick wealth is like an intense lust which demands a quick love. Gambling and intense lust both are sisterhoods of war, in my opinion". You mocked me by repeating "founded on lust and fortune," giggling.

"I don't buy and sell human beings," that's what Rick Blaine said in Casablanca. Sometimes dreams move beyond dreaming, beyond the dream's nature. Yes, you may laugh at me and ask, *"What do you mean by the nature of dreams?"* It's like what I told you one day, "I really miss the public payphone booths. I miss reading the words on the walls of those old phone booths. Because I can imagine how someone had made such scribbles in payphone booths when he or she had been listening to a busy tone." I mean such an old doodling had always made me think of someone who has been eagerly looking for a response, but probably has never received it. A response like an intimate gaze or a short intimate talk that is needed for survival. Like what a man talked to me after my IELTS exam. Like the moments we were watching Casablanca together.

No, I didn't force you to watch it, maybe I bribed you with some chips and dip and a bottle of wine to company me.

You asked me, "Why are you crying?" Was I really crying? I don't remember that. But I remember you were laughing at me. I just remember Casablanca was showing the scene where the goodbye letter was getting totally wet by rain in the hands of Rick Blaine, and the ink of words was flowing with raindrops on the letter. "I don't buy and sell human beings," that's what I remember Rick Blaine said in Casablanca.

---

* *Casablanca is a 1942 American movie directed by Michael Curtiz.*

LUMINESCENT

When my children started going to kindergarten, still new immigrants, every holiday, I had to answer their questions; "Who are our grandparents? Why don't we go to their home for this event, while others do?" The only true answer was they passed away. But what I was not able to answer was, so why don't we bring some flowers to their tombs, or something like that? And I could hear some nonverbalized questions too; *Are you just lying about their existence?* and I could see in the depth of their eyes the question, *"What am I attached to as proof of myself?"* Wellbeing was not proved yet. Something still beyond all other materials was needed. Something evident.

I love getting lost in reveries. My physician sees it as traumatic, but I enjoy sleeping. I laugh. He frowns and prescribes a pill. "Why do I need it? What does it do to me?" I ask. "It makes you awaken like a work dog," he answers. I murmur "Like a pain killer." The pharmacist says the same thing: "awaken like a work dog." I thanked her, but later I threw that pill in the trash bin on my way home.

I go to bed and after some minutes struggling myself, I fall asleep. I have a dream; I see myself in front of my childhood home (I don't know why I see this house always immersed in the moonlight of a calm night). My mom opens the door. I kiss her many times happily.

I wake up to go to the washroom, then I cannot sleep anymore.

As a five-year-old boy, I found that the phosphorescent prayer beads of a rosery worked as a wonderful toy to keep me distracted from my sick Grandma at night. Mom whispered to Leyla; her hired help, "Keep him away from here…entertain him," and then talked to herself, "Entertain? … in this dark night?" It was an overwhelming time when my mom had my newborn sister and my sick Grandma, and she had to take care of both, with other responsibilities including me, a small child. Dad was overwhelmed too. Working as the schoolmaster with two little children and a sick mother in the unstable situation of our country because of the revolution and a war.

Leyla came out to the garden and called me as if she had found something very joyful. She opened her arms as if she was going to hug me. "Come, come and see what is going on here." I ran to the steps, and she held my hand. "Come, it's here … I picked a star from the sky!"

We walked to the other side of the house. There was a long opening in front of a room which we normally used for reception of the guests. "Close your eyes and don't open them till I tell you," Leyla said. I closed my eyes and then I heard the whispers of waving trees in the breeze of that warm night. I could hear the rustling of leaves and some far sounds of animals and people. And this time I could hear the sounds as if I had never heard them.

"Now open your eyes," Leyla said. I opened my eyes and saw a luminous dot turning in a bowl of water. I was fascinated. "A star in a bowl of water! Where did it come from?" I asked joyfully. Leyla put her finger on the luminous dot and moved it to turn around in the bowl. After a few minutes when that luminous dot started to lose its glow, Leyla took it out of water to breathe onto it like when she was warming her hands in the winter. And when it was returned to the bowl of water, it glowed again. I was excited to turn the luminous dot and warm it too, like Leyla did. "Why only one star? Where are the other stars?" I asked as I was turning my head toward the sky. But in turning my head, I saw several luminous dots of Leyla's necklace. Her necklace was a set of prayer beads that my grandma had given to her, and she never used it for counting prayers the way Grandma did. Instead, Leyla used to wear the prayer beads as a necklace. She laughed and hastily she covered her necklace with her collar. Then, she turned the luminous dot in the bowl of water faster than before to make a luminous circle. "Look!" she said.

TO MEET IN AN UNSEEN END

It's about 10:00 pm on Sunday in early summer in one of the rooms of a luxury hotel in a rich city in the Netherlands. A young Iranian man is looking down from his window. He watches the city, the flickering lights of night clubs at the far end of the street, cars on the highways, and the changing colors of traffic lights in the closer cross sections. Two small pieces of luggage are left on the floor beside the bed, one unopened yet, and the other one opened with some women's clothes and cosmetics in it. An Iranian girl is seated on the edge of the window that the man is watching the city through and is concentrating on her writing in a notebook. They have made love in this room this evening after having their dinner in a good restaurant close by.

"What are you writing about so seriously?" the man asks.

"Nothing, something to relax myself."

"I have never seen you write anything in our previous meetings."

"You haven't seen it, yet it doesn't mean that I have not done this before," she says while she is still concentrating on her writing. And the man watches the city without any particular purpose. Then he asks, "Well, what is that about? Why didn't you show it to me till now?"

"I opened my notebook tonight first because I needed it. And second, I thought you were grown up enough to understand that it is something private."

The man repeats "something private" sarcastically.

"Yes private, and if you still don't understand it, I will put it back in my luggage, like the other nights."

The man playfully tries to snatch the notebook. But the girl quickly closes the notebook and jumps down from the window's edge. She quickly takes guard as if she is ready for a serious fight.

The man is caught off guard and tries to control the situation with laughter and prank.

"OK, I am grown up after these six months…well…I just wanted to see what you are writing about."

"Not six months yet, and only every other weekend…so far only twelve weekends."

"WOW, you have counted it so precisely. Is it your accounting book?" The man laughs heavily.

The girl looks frustrated. "Hahaha…not as easy as you think. I have not come here as an international student like you who has failed his courses but still has money to live."

"No, I'm not an international student anymore. You know that. It was several years ago. And now I'm working to make my living. There is no financial support anymore."

"Congratulations, but still, you talk about your scholarship sometimes."

The man goes slowly toward the bed and sits on the edge of it, looking down on the carpet and two pieces of luggage. The girl returns to the edge of the window. She sits there and bends one of her legs to use it like her desk, and the other leg hangs toward the floor.

Then the girl comes down and puts on her pants and her t-shirt and gets herself ready to go outside.

"Where do you go?"

"Outside. For a smoke."

"I'm coming with you. Wait a second."

"But you don't smoke. Do you?"

"I want to accompany you." He puts on his pants and shirt too. "Maybe you could share your cigarette with me." He smiles softly.

"OK. Come." She grabs her notebook too.

Outside of the hotel in a green area, they sit on a bench and share a cigarette silently.

"Read something from your notebook…please."

She reads, "A battered heart can still fall in love. You might say, "You made it eventually". But I stroll in my memories all the time talking to an imaginary companion. Companionship is a need. One day you said, "Dogs are different than most other animals, they have always been living with human beings. It's part of their life. Although they can survive without living with human beings, probably they are happier in this way…a happy life is more than just survival."

"What is that about?" The man looks depressed.

"It's my memoir."

"What kind of memories are these?"

"It's the diary of a romantic whore." She says and looks at the man with contempt.

The man feels angry. "You know that word makes me nervous…I told you many times."

The girl puffs her cigarette silently and embraces her knees with both arms. The man gestures to ask her to pass it back to him.

They spend several moments just puffing their cigarette silently. Then the man askes politely, "Tell me something real."

"All I have told you is real…You and I only meet each other to spend one night in a luxury hotel or motel every other weekend. In the past five-ish months. That's it. There is nothing more for me and I don't expect anything from such a relationship. That's the way you feel empowered. And certainly, such a relationship doesn't put you in a legal trap. You are safe baby…you don't need to take any serious responsibility."

"I work hard in a factory for two weeks to save enough money for just one or two precious nights."

"I know that, and I can imagine in what type of residences you live in the rest of days."

"…Let's forget about the other nights…"

"Why? Do you think you can fool a life?"

The man looks too weak. He pleads, "Read your diary… instead of prying into my daily life."

"How often do you wash your clothes?"

The man doesn't seem well, he cannot concentrate on his words too, but he asks, "And you? What about you?" The girl leaves the bench to sit on the grass in front of the man. She smokes and talks slowly and calmly.

"I was raised by my grandmother. Have never seen my parents. I have no memory of them. My grandma died after I graduated from high school ten years ago. She had hoped to see my marriage. Lucky and happy. It was her only wish in her life. She was always saying that her house belonged to me, and she wanted me to live there with my husband. But she died a few months after my graduation before anyone knocks on our door for proposal.

Later a man came and proposed me. He was more than twenty years older than me. But he was good looking and a strong man. He was a truck driver. He used to work for a transportation company, transporting goods across Iran and sometimes internationally. He said if we get married, he knows a way for us to go to the USA but first we need to move to the Netherlands. Probably he was hoping that such inspiring ideas would help me to love him and cope with the difficulties of his job. It was like a sweet dream. Going to Europe or the USA. I had no clear idea about foreign countries. I just had a few trips to Tehran with my grandma. Even those few trips had been enough to create a great desire in my heart to live in big cities. I loved to collect photos of different cities from any brochure or magazine I could find. I had a big notebook that I had used as my collection of those photos. I had a true feeling that the differences between what I could imagine through such photos and my boring daily life enshrouded with rules and traditions was huge. But I had no idea about what the basis of such differences was. My mind was far away from such questions and answers.

We came to the Netherlands eventually. My husband started his job in a transportation company. But after a few months I received a very bad news, he died because of heart attack during one of his trips."

The man is bent on his knees now. Embraces his arms with his hands, "Probably because of drinking alcohol."

"He was healthy and strong I believe…mmm…he was a smoker too."

"Read more…please." The man seems helpless and unable to move. The girl reads while she shares her second smoke with the man.

"We had each decided to go from one side of the hill and meet each other again at the other side of the hill. It looked exciting.

We had assumed that we would each go through a semicircle. But we did not know that we had assumed that these semicircles were similar. And we did not know that we had assumed that these semicircles would meet their ends at the same point on the other side of the hill. And we did not know that we had assumed that we both would reach there at the same time.

I did not know how your path was and how did you go about that. But as soon as I set off, I realized that I had a difficult and rocky road ahead. Perhaps this difficulty was due to walking alone. But I kept looking at the curvature of the hill as if, as soon as I reached there, the road would reach its end, and I would see you there again. But the curvature never reached its end. It continued and appeared as a new curve again and again. Then I decided to run faster. Assuming all roads will reach their end sooner if I run faster. Maybe I was terrified. Little by little, my legs were injured by rocks and thorns. I was tired. I was also thirsty. But this curvature had no end. It was as if the semicircles would never meet at an assumed meeting point. I was thirsty and tired. I saw a tree away from the path I was walking. I assumed there must be a spring of water. A place where I can drink and rest. I was hopeful of being able to walk the curve of the hill later. When I reached the tree, I was more tired and thirsty. But there was neither a stream nor a pond. I was completely exhausted. I wanted to break a branch to make a cane to help me walk. I had to climb the tree. I climbed one step. And then another step. And after taking another step, I saw a better view of the hill and the road. Just then I realized that the hill never ends. But next to it, there were other small and big hills piled up like an infinite series of small and big pieces of rubble. I realized that I was not even able to tell exactly where I was, or to point to the hill that I had left it to go toward the tree. I thought that I had to go back to our starting point. The point where we had separated to take our own ways. But coming back to the first point was even harder than going ahead. I had no other choice than to move on."

The man is shivering now. "And what happened after that?"

The girl holds the man's arm to pull him up and helps him stand straight. "You are shivering...Let's go back to our room... Are you feeling cold?"

"No. I want to know more." The man says.

"It seems you are faint after this smoke...You might get sick if we stay here longer...I will tell you in our way back." The man shivers and walks slowly. The girl still holds his arm like a wife.

"Then I was searching for a way to make my living. One day I went to a community center. I was not even able to speak English. An old lady who was working there called one of her co-workers who was Iranian too. The Iranian lady helped me as an interpreter between me and that old lady. The old lady asked me, "So, how have you come to this country?" I was shocked and terrified. I thought that she wanted to kick me out of her country. But the interpreter said, "No, she is not an immigration officer, she just needs to know your situation. So, why did you and your husband leave Iran?" I said we thought we deserved a better life. Is it illegal? The interpreter said, no it's your right to improve your lifestyle if work for it. Her words made me very happy, and I cried out, "Yes! I didn't know that it was my right! I want to use my right!...I want to keep my right!"

And at this point in her story, the girl laughed involuntarily like a little child.

The man and the girl leave the elevator and walk toward their room. The man still shivers.

In the room, they both sit on the edge of the bed. The man needs a glass of wine, and the girl pours the remains of the bottle in two glasses. They drink silently. The girl watches the city through the window and the man watches the girl's body and the reflection of her body in the glass of window. He can barely distinguish between the reflections and the real body. He feels bad, like the feeling of a child on the last night of his holiday season. Nervous and deprived.

The man lays on his left side on the bed, cringed, embraces his knees, like a fetus in the mother's womb.

The girl covers him with a blanket and turns the sidelight of the bed off, like a mother.

She comes back to the edge of window and sits there. She bends one of her legs to use it like her desk, and the other leg hangs toward the floor. She writes:

"A battered heart can still feel love as a necessity" I said. And you replied, "like what dogs probably feel, in my opinion".

"And now I can say like wolves instead. Although wolves are also from the same family as dogs. But wolves will come back from hunting with mouths full of salty blood and the feverish bodies covered by sweat of a summer night when eventually they have become thirsty. They need to feel a breeze while they are mating under moonlight. They need to come back for mating. They come back for a sip of cold water in the same creek that a deer has run away from in a bloody evening."

"Wolves are more careful about their freedom than dogs. Wolves keep themselves happy too. But they choose their companions first. There are two groups of wolves. The first group runs for hunting. To taste the blood and flesh. And the second group have become wolves to stay and nurture."

"After the failure of all attempts at survival, the inner power for life floods in again. This time the flood of liveliness appears monstrously powerful. It comes as love."

AND STILL BURNING

We — my colleague and I —were in Rome in the mid-90s. We travelled there as the engineering team of an Iranian project to work with a vendor. The Iran-Iraq war had ended, and some industrial projects had been re-started in Iran. As soon as we arrived and were settled in our hotel, my colleague, whom I will call "Hypocrite," started talking to me about his dreams of drinking and seeking enjoyment during our short working period in Rome, although he acted ridiculously composed when we were in front of our bosses or other coworkers. You probably know what I mean....

One Friday evening when we were back at the hotel, he started saying: "It's our weekend, let's go to a bar and a beautiful cabaret, it's our free time, why not?"

He knew that I drank occasionally. Eventually, we went to a bar close to our hotel. After some drinks he insisted on finding other places. I tried to tease him and said we should go to Campo de' Fiori.

"Where is it?" Hypocrite asked.

"It's a very beautiful place and it is the place where Giordano Bruno was burnt alive," I said, but Hypocrite didn't believe me and assumed I was joking. Then I started to explain Giordano Bruno and the Dark Ages. "Such people were sacrificed to teach us how to think," I said.

He still thought I was joking, although I was serious. We left the bar discussing Campo de' Fiori, Giordano Bruno, and the Dark Ages. I dumped on him all I had read about humanity and the history of philosophy, and, shamefully, I thought I knew a lot.

We reached a cinema. We were probably talking animatedly and loudly in Farsi for we attracted the attention of a man who was putting up photos on the theatre wall.

He turned to us and said sardonically in Farsi: "Gentlemen, please calm down." It was an invitation to the conversation.

He looked like Omar Sharif in Dr. Zhivago, so I will call him The Doctor. When we started talking together, I realized that the Doctor was overwhelmed and had been looking for a moment of rest after a long working day. But soon he wanted to leave and said that his working time was over, and that he had to rush to see a sick relative.

I asked him to drive us to Campo de' Fiori since he had finished working and we were ready to pay him for the drive. In the car I sat in front beside the driver. Hypocrite was in the backseat. Hypocrite, apparently drunk, asked the Doctor to drive us somewhere enjoyable. I was interested to know about the Doctor's life and why he was living in Rome, but I realized he was hesitant to talk in front of Hypocrite, assuming the latter was spying on him.

When I asked the Doctor about his life, instead of an answer he asked me: "Why are you interested in Campo De' Fiori?" and again I tried to impress him with all I had read.

The Doctor said, "I have read some of these books too...I was a communist...I escaped after 1980...You might have heard about that time."

I wanted to know more but he was reticent. After more questions and trying to reassure and relax him, he continued to speak vaguely; I understood he had been a university student but had to escape from Iran because of his ideology and having participated in protests with other students at the university against restrictions enforced by the religious revolutionary government. And after several months of living in that troubled time, he had been lucky to arrive in Italy. Now he was working as a handy man in different places and his job in that cinema was the cleanest one.

"Your energy," he said, "when you were talking about the Dark Ages, reminded me of those days after 1979 in Iran and political arguments with my friends." His political activities had been limited to distributing some newspapers and participating in some political gatherings. That was the extent of all the political activities he had done in Iran or elsewhere.

Then he asked me again: "Why are you interested in seeing Campo de' Fiori?"

I explained that I wanted to open the eyes of Hypocrite, but he replied with a cynical smile.

After a long drive we arrived in an area that did not seem very beautiful or comfortable. The street was lined with apartments. He parked the car and said, "Follow me."

After climbing a long staircase, we reached a tiny apartment. He opened the door and we entered. The apartment was filled with the smell of fever and sickness. A sick skinny lady was lying on the bed burning with fever.

The Doctor said, "There you go, here is Campo de' Fiori...and the burning Giordano Bruno...See? ... He is still burning." Some copies of a book in a foreign language that I was unable to read were piled beside the lady's bed.

"Who is she?" I asked as I took one of the books.

"She is a refugee from the Balkan war. Don't you know that a brutal war is ongoing there? She was a writer and escaped from this horrible war between formerly communist armies. Like me, a communist student who escaped from a religious country."

Hypocrite was badly agitated and shouted at me angrily, "Let's leave now!"

But I wanted to know more. I looked at the book, a green cover with a portrait of that lady on the title page. For a few seconds I felt that I drowned in nothingness, floating nowhere.

Hypocrite left the apartment. He rushed down the stairs scolding me and went out into the street. I wanted to give the Doctor some money, but he looked at me sadly. I felt ashamed. I collected myself and said, "I want to pay for this book...I want to buy a copy."

"You cannot read it, I cannot read it either. Why do you want to buy it?" said the Doctor.

"Oh, yes. I even want to buy two copies, one for myself and one for my colleague," I said. The Doctor looked through the window and said, "For him? A book?"

We looked out at the street and saw that Hypocrite was vomiting into a garbage bin.

We left the apartment. The Doctor was ready to take us back to our hotel because we were very far, and it would be difficult for us to return at that late hour.

"What about that sick woman?" I asked.

"She will be sleeping by the time I get back," said the Doctor.

After vomiting, Hypocrite berated me saying: "You ruined my night…Campo de' Fiori…Campo de' Fiori."

In the car, Hypocrite rambled on in the backseat with unstoppable hiccups.

The Doctor was loquacious, probably because his heart was eagerly looking for an intimate conversation. He was speaking about the refugees of Balkan, and said, "I don't believe in communism anymore and I don't believe in any religion. Probably all I wanted as a student at university during the days of revolution was justice, which I couldn't find anywhere."

Between hiccups, Hypocrite grumbled that I had ruined his night by continually saying, "Campo de' Fiori… what a night! Campo de' Fiori…What a stupid friend!"

I felt I was sitting between two ruined lives, two ruined worlds, one who was driving the car and the other who lolled on the backseat seeking enjoyment. Sitting between one who was self-censoring his words, and the other who was nagging and hiccupping. It started to drizzle.

After a long pause the Doctor asked me, "Do you… still want to go to Campo de' Fiori?"

I didn't answer, I didn't have an answer. I closed my eyes so as not to see the striking row of streetlights running fast towards us and smashing on the windshield through the rain drops and the darkness of night.

TRANSPLANTED

One Saturday afternoon in Toronto while I was bathing, my wife hurried in, agitated, and called to me where I stood behind the shower curtain.

"She came again," said my wife. "She said it makes more gardening work for her. What gardening work might it cause for her?"

My wife was talking about a Persian walnut tree that a friend brought us from Niagara Falls. Four or five years ago on a wet and rainy spring afternoon, he came to our backyard, laughing happily. He was coming back from Niagara Falls with two tiny branches in his car.

"Persian Walnut, you see...one for you and one for me," said our friend while planting one of the tiny branches in the corner of our backyard. We used to watch it while seated at the kitchen table, watching it grow and spread, attracting the squirrels that were claiming its branches and chewing its leaves, until it became tall enough to peep over the fence.

Then two weeks ago, our backyard neighbor called my wife and said, "Cut this tree down, it is making more gardening work for me." She was the wife of an old, retired policeman.

My wife tried to convince her. "We will take care of everything, and it will not bother you at all," she said, but her words had no success. We sat at the kitchen table thinking about what we could do. While I was cutting two branches which were closest to the neighbor's fence, my wife was talking almost to herself. "I teach the children in kindergarten about how we should respect Mother Earth, the beauty of nature...What work does it make for her?"

After the second warning from the neighbor lady, we became desperate. We couldn't even sit at the kitchen table. My wife rushed to the garage and came back with a shovel. She muttered angrily, digging fast, and beating and hitting the ground. I tried to take the shovel from her hand.

"We will transplant it," said my wife.

We extracted the plant from the backyard. We had to cut some roots and some branches and leaves to fit it in the trunk.

"I will keep these branches and leaves for art activities for my students," my wife said again muttering without looking at me.

My wife drove faster than normal and honked her horn, something she normally did not do. We drove north to the summer house of our friend who had given us the tree.

I was looking at my worried nervous wife, but we did not exchange words. Memories of the past engulfed me.

When I was a young adult, I met one of my high school teachers after a couple of years. A middle-aged man who had retired recently. Or had been forced to retire. Why? Because not all revolutionary ideas can succeed. Especially when the dictatorship is tied to international economic desires. That's what he said when I met him in his backyard in early autumn. He was working around the plants in his small garden. In fact, he had no specific plan; he was only entertaining himself. Why? To forget his troubles. He had been kicked out of a job that he had loved and spent all his energy on when he was young. Furthermore, his wife was sick. Maybe because of the many stressors around her family. I knew that she had been traveling between home and hospital for the past few months. I strolled with my teacher around his backyard while we chatted. It was early autumn. The weather was cold, especially in the late afternoons and nights. Leaves had started to change colors and many of them had already fallen. Suddenly something attracted my teacher's attention. It was one of the plants in the corner of his backyard. It was a small plant that had a flower like a rooster's crown. I'm not sure if its name was really rooster's crown or not, but we called it "rooster's crown" that afternoon. The rooster's crown seemed to have risen suddenly although its leaves were crumpled. It had dried up in that area which had no rainy days most of the year. At the same time, it had risen and grown its seeds. My teacher bent to the rooster's crown and sat beside it. He looked intently at the rooster's crown. He started caressing the wilted leaves of the flower, murmuring, "See how it has grown its seeds suddenly. It always happens in this season. When the plant feels cold in dry land, it understands that it is going to die, then immediately grows its seeds. Its last bit of energy becomes a seed. What is the mystery behind this? Isn't it the enthusiasm for the continuation of life? Does this plant understand that it will be dead soon? Does it understand that it must grow new seedlings to continue?" Apparently, my teacher was not talking to me only. Was he looking inwardly at his own body? He turned his face to me and said, "Yes, freedom and life reproduction are interrelated."

I heard later that he immigrated to another country with his family. I worried if his sick wife would be able to heal and survive their long journey.

Hesitantly, with some unreasonable shame, we approached our friend. He laughed and joked as if he wanted to smooth the air. My wife wouldn't let me take the shovel. She shoveled the ground, beating and hitting it, and eventually we transplanted the Persian walnut tree that late October. We poured plenty of water onto it and added vitamin pills to its injured roots before we returned home.

We were seated at the kitchen table, drinking our coffee. "Will it survive?" my wife asked, staring out into nowhere. "Ye...yes it will," I answered.

A COT

I was browsing through the messenger on my cellphone when I saw this message following a lovely photo of a flower from one of my Italian friends in Toronto.

"Years ago, a friend gave me a weak, dying plant. I did not know where it came from nor her name.

"I planted her in the yard and waited. The first ten years passed without her growing even one meter. Ten years passed yet she still seemed weak and dying. Her branches were getting broken every year. She had no flowers and no shadow nor perfume."

"I watered her many times in despair and tied her to the fence to help her not to fall on the ground.

"Sometimes some people did not hesitate to show their astonishment and ridicule by saying, "What is this? Cut it and leave it to die."

"Until she erupted two years ago. She grew tall and covered the eastern fence of the house. She started to bloom and showed her blossoms. She cleverly and bravely pervaded her lovely perfume over our backyard. She gave us such beautiful flowers that were attracting the pedestrians to turn their heads for a glance or even to stand for a deeper look and a breath."

"This year, however, she grew more than before with a mass of flowers. Could you believe it, she attracts and feeds thousands of bees everyday now?"

Then I moved to another message. A new one, like an unknown friend. But the message looked very familiar. When I looked closely, I realized that the message was advertising a cot for sale. An old-style cot that you might only see something like that in the WWII movies or in your frayed memories.

One day in early summer when I was a student in elementary school, we tried to take it out from beneath other old stuff loaded in that room. It was laid against the wall and some other stuff like carpets and boxes were laid on top of it. First it seemed to us like a gun. A buttstock with some pieces of black metal on it. "There you go, something for fun." It seemed an interesting thing for a hot summer day when I should not go to school. I thought I could pull it out easily with some help from my little sister. My sister was not old enough, so she was not able to help much. But we both tried to pull it out. I had never seen a gun in our house. My sister was giggling. "Stop giggling, and just go to the other side and push, so, one,…two…"

My sister fell on her back and started giggling again. We did not ask for help from anybody. If we were asking for help, then what was the fun? But it seemed longer than a gun. And taking it out was not as easy as I initially thought. Anyway, we were halfway pulling it out, so pushing it back was even harder. And eventually, it rambled out. Four pieces of wood and each two pieces had been hinged together like a giant X. We turned it and there was the same set of hinged wood and a sheet of very thick fabric connected to both sets of giant X. Now we started to push it out of the room. Then we pushed it to bring it into the hall. The hall was just a bigger room, in the middle of the building with four doors. Two doors were opening the hall to two sides of the house yard. And the other two doors on each side of the hall were opening to the other two rooms of the house.

Until we moved it to the hall, the hinges were turned, and the giant X expanded like a bench or probably like a bed.

When we looked up Mom and Dad were standing in the yard in the front of the hall door gawking at us. Dad seemed angry, he came in and said, "Didn't you think it is a dangerous thing? You might hurt yourself with its hinges."

I was wondering why dad was overreacting, since that giant X and fabric didn't seem a dangerous thing, its hinges did not pinch our fingers, and we were not hurt at all. Mom explained to us that it's a cot and it's not a toy, then she took us away to give us some fruit and find another entertainment for us.

After half an hour I sneaked back. The cot was still in the hall and my dad was lying on it. He had bent one arm on his forehead, one of his feet straight and the other foot bent. The fabric of that cot sagged under his body. I was unable to understand why he seemed younger in that position. He still had his shoes on. I had never seen him in bed with his shoes before. Was he asleep? No, he was murmuring a song, something like a military march.

Years later, when the cot had been totally forgotten, my sister had been married, and my dad passed away. My mom, who was old then, and not strong enough to take care of our old house, decided to move to another house, a new style and smaller house. I saw that cot again, when we were packaging our things to take them into the new house. I didn't want to touch it. I had a bad feeling about that cot. Because I had been told that it was a dangerous thing. Mom, then told me that I have a late uncle, older than my dad, who has been a good strong lad. When my dad was just a young boy, my uncle was assumed to be the caregiver of my dad and my aunt, because my grandpa had passed away in those days. My uncle had gone to WWII and that cot was the only thing back.

III
ELSEWHERE

SILENT TUNING FORKS

Years ago, when I was working on a large project, I went to a foreign country to inspect the giant electric motors that are only produced in a small handful of factories across the world. I went to a big factory that produced a lot of things in a small town with many workers and employees who were moving and working like ants. Workshops like matchboxes stacked next to each other here and there, and the roads that had them connected. The head office had been located like a temple atop a hill close to the gate of that factory. Although it had been fabricating sophisticated products with advanced technology, it did not seem to be an attractive environment at all. The workers all looked gloomy and depressed. No trees or flowers were seen anywhere except a few around the head office. The colour of workers' clothes was mostly gray or pale green, like the color of the cars and the color of the doors and walls of the workshops. Strict and inflexible rules were applying there even to me, who came there from a large project as their client.

A senior employee came to the head office and, after reminding me of a series of regulations, took me with him to a workshop where I was going to inspect some electrical equipment. And he had to stay there until the end of inspection process and then return me with the same car. His seriousness, along with his exaggerated respect, seemed to me very funny. From time to time, he was trying to insist on the ability of their factory to account for any work or production that I was inspecting. His behavior and words were making me laugh, but of course I would not be laughing at him because it was considered rude.

Eventually my job was done, and the senior employee and I got in the car to drive back to the exit gate. On the way between the workshop and the gate we had to pass several roads, and in the middle of the road, a trailer came out of one of the workshops and started driving in front of our car very slowly and cautiously. The senior employee looked at me with a smile and said, "They

69

don't seem to know we're in a hurry." I felt that he wanted to test my patience, but in fact all my gaze and attention had been drawn to the shape of the things that had been loaded into the trailer. Numerous metallic tubes that had been very well cut and perfectly polished. Like cylindrical mirrors in several different sizes. Short and long. Fat and thin. I was just staring at the beauty of these cylinders. They seemed very beautiful, although they were only simple cylinders. But I was thinking that these simple, shiny cylinders had been stacked together and neatly packaged as if wrapped in white ribbons like gifts. I fancied that they were stacked together like a big musical instrument. They had seemed to be like one of those toys that produced melodies when you played with them. I remember that I had broken one of them when I was a child. Inside that broken toy was a revolving cylinder that had some prominent points which hit the bars to produce music. Those melodical toys that we enjoyed a lot as a child. The same velvety songs that smelled like vanilla and biscuit flavor.

I reviewed in my mind the similarity of these cylinders and bars and the natural frequency of each, then I said, "Like a giant pipe organ." "No, they can't vibrate," the senior employee said with a proud smile. "But they each have a natural frequency, like a tuning fork, an acoustic resonator with a natural frequency," I replied and emphasized the word "natural" to remind him of a physical phenomenon when I answered. But he said, "No, we will install them according to a special design," and he insisted, "A *special* design. All will be installed deep in the sea and in a concrete enclosure. Yes, they have a natural frequency. But we designed it to neutralize all the vibrations and fluctuations of the water waves for thirty years without moving." I confess that my knowledge of steel structures is very poor, but I could guess that these metallic tubes were designed for an oil rig in the sea. "And what will happen after thirty years?" I asked, and the senior employee replied, "We will dismantle them and recycle their metal, we have a contract for thirty years."

As he was explaining, suddenly some of the packaging became unwrapped, and cylinders fell from the trailer with a sound like

70

chiming bells and rolled on the ground. The surprised and angry senior employee stopped the car and ran to inform the trailer driver about what had happened. Then he called the workers to collect the cylinders. He came back to our car after he had done his investigations and provided instructions to the workers. He told me anxiously, "I am very sorry, but you need to get out of the car. Please wait here on the sidewalk. I must go back to another office and help to return these things to the workshop." I felt that he meant the workers and the cylinders all together when he said "these". Then he continued, "Please stay here and do not move, I've called another car to come and drive you to the exit gate." His saying "stay here" again made me laugh. But obviously I did not laugh at all. I thought that his words were meant as if I had to wait there, standing still, until I become recycled according to the contract.

MINGLING

You arrive at a hotel in the suburb of Johannesburg in the evening. The hotel does not serve dinner and it is too late to go outside alone, especially in a place totally new to you. You lay down in bed hoping to fall asleep.

A tent of silence is expanded everywhere, and any short sigh or crunch can be heard. Is it moaning or giggling in the next room? The crinkling sound of someone opening a biscuit, perhaps. Indistinct chatter. Soft talk? Maybe, but nothing comprehensible. You can only hear some sounds. The sound of tapping, like the running of a dog, maybe, but you have not heard any barking.

More soft voices? The sound of hands moving around the bed sheet. The sound of walking? Maybe. The sound of water (or another beverage?) pouring in a glass. The sound of moaning again. Moaning? Maybe, but certainly not a sad voice. Indistinct chattering as if someone is lip-reading or whispering, but no words can be heard, just the sound of pursing lips. You fall asleep. You do not know how long you have been asleep. But you are awake now. Are you awake because you are starving? Or because of jet lag? Maybe. Or because you can hear the voice of your neighbor again? Or neighbors? You are awake and you can hear a couple (a couple?) in the next room making love. (Or are they?) You are starving. You are sure you are disturbed because of jet lag, and you are tired from a long travel. You probably fall asleep again.

It is morning. Is it morning? Maybe. You want to hasten for breakfast before it is over. You hear your neighbour (neighbours?) moving, as if they are putting on their clothes to get ready for breakfast. Is it not too late for breakfast? Maybe not. You will get ready hastily. Is it because you are too hungry? Or maybe you are a nosy person, and you want to discover who your neighbour is (are?). But for sure you are not nosy. It is your curiosity that moves you to figure out what is going on in your surroundings. You feel

72

that you need to talk to someone. You need a moment of chatting, drinking, and laughing. And as a human being you need to share your empathy with someone.

You leave the room but still your neighbours have not left their room. You come back and stay behind the door of your room. You did not do anything bad for sure. It is your room anyway. You can stand behind the door of your room as if you are ready to go for breakfast. Or in the meantime you can look at yourself in the mirror of the bathroom which is not far from the door. You hear that someone opens the door of the next room. You open the door too, slowly, and cautiously. You go gently to the corridor. A couple come out of the next room. You stand as a gentleman to let them move ahead of you in the corridor.

The lady and the man from the next room move ahead. The man holds a white cane in his left hand, and his right hand is in the left hand of the lady. The man has worn sunglasses. And the lady is moving her lips as if she is lip reading into the ear of the man. You say, "Good Morning." Only the man replies and apparently the lady has not heard anything. They move ahead and you follow them in the corridor toward the dining room of the hotel. Are they giggling? Maybe. But it looks like they are carefully listening to something outside of the building.

You slowly follow them to the dining room of the hotel that only serves breakfast. They take their coffee first and hand in hand go to sit at a table close to a wide window. There are not many tables in the dining room and most of them are occupied, so you find an excuse to ask this lovely couple if you can take a seat beside them. They happily welcome you.

After bringing your coffee and sitting down at the table you say, "The smell of this coffee is wonderful." The man smiles and agree with you and the lady turns her cup of coffee below her nose and smiles kindly.

A big bird appears roaming on the grassland of the hotel not too far from the building. The lady touches the hand of the man, and both turn their faces toward the window to look at the bird. The man says, "A Hadeda is on the grassland." And, turns to his wife, "Apparently, we are lucky. Hopefully we can take good videos and photos of them."

You repeat while you are looking at the bird through the window, "Hadeda...Ha...de...da".

The man says, "Yes, exactly, Ha...de...da, this bird is named because of its specific sound...three repetitive notes." He repeats Hadeda rhythmically and his wife synchronously taps with her finger on the table. Then both wife and husband giggle again.

You say, "Oh, you are biologist I guess." Now, the man touches the hand of the lady and says, "My wife is a professional painter, I am a freelance researcher in the field of birds and ecology."

While the man explains the proficiency of him and his wife, his wife looks passionately at her husband. The man continues, "My wife wants to take some videos and photos to present the new views of Hadeda life. Hadeda have some interesting behaviors, they can track the gaze of people around them to monitor their safety." The lady then moves her eyes from one side to another with a fascinating smile to express what her husband says about tracking the gaze of human beings by Hadeda, and then she moves her hand as if a bird or an airplane takes off suddenly.

You say, "That's quite a unique behavior, I guess. That should be their defense mechanism."

The man – the freelance biologist – says, "not a unique behavior, but certainly not very common in birds. However, Hadeda has a very interesting lifestyle. For instance, they don't mind if human beings get close to them. Another important fact that I am currently researching is that Hadeda are monogamous."

You express your surprise and ask, "Is it a defense mechanism too?"

"That's a good question," the man replies and continues, "How could we prove it?" and both him and his wife giggle. You giggle too, then as if you have found the answer to a dilemma, you reply happy and assertive, "There should not be an evolutionary reason considered for the monogamy of Hadeda."

"How do you know that?" The man asks and both him and his wife giggle again.

"If there were an evolutionary reason as a defense mechanism for being monogamous then all human beings would be monogamous in their nature too because we, human beings, are the most successful species." You explain with enough confidence when you and your kind and happy friends have almost finished your breakfast. Then they look at each other passionately, and the man asks, "Are you sure that we – human beings – are the most successful species?"

SEQUENTIAL HARMS

It was about ten years ago that Mr. B immigrated to Canada. In Iran, he had graduated with a master's degree in English literature. He taught for a while as a supply teacher, but he had also worked in a lathe workshop. It was a job that he used to do when he was still a high school student and in parallel with his studies at the university. Mr. B was very interested in literature, especially English literature. He had read many English literary works. He had learned the criticism and the opinions of great writers about English literary works in an academic manner. I was introduced to Mr. B by his sister's husband, Mr. K, my friend. Mr. K knew that I liked to talk about English literature with someone knowledgeable in this field. In addition, he was attempting to change Mr. B's mood through this acquaintance. In fact, Mr. B was very depressed. Mr. B and his wife were separated after a long disastrous argument, and she had also taken their little son away from him.

Mr. B had been seriously involved in political movements in 1979, when he was a high school student. It is not possible to say with certainty that his interest in politics made him study literature so carefully or vice versa. In any case, Mr. B was arrested and tortured due to his fervent activity in a political party whose activities were banned soon after the religious Revolution of 1979. Although he was one of the thousands of young students who tried with all their might for the victory of the Revolution of 1979.

In all stages of interrogation and torture, he had tried to stay loyal to his party and not reveal anything about his group members. Nonetheless, this sacrifice was useless because one day after a tough interrogation, the interrogator (or interrogators) confronted him with one of the leaders of his party. That person, who was one of the people above him, had exposed not only Mr. B, but also all the other members of the party. After that humiliating scene,

Mr. B was transferred from solitary confinement to a general prison where he was imprisoned with his party members and several others who were all older than him. This was, of course, to learn the ways of correct behavior from his elders. The dictatorship carved scars on the deepest layer of his personality.

Mr. B was lucky enough to get out of prison alive, continue his studies, graduate from university, and find a part-time job teaching. He also continued to work in a lathe workshop, despite the usual opposition and obstacles in his way. I think that everything was done by his family to save him from the harms of imprisonment. His family and all his relatives around him had done whatever they were able to do, even an arrangement for marriage that made him the father of a child too.

In Canada, he found a low-paying job in a small Persian restaurant, and after more effort, he found a labor job in a lathe workshop near Kingston. This was the time when I approached him to talk about English literature, when he was in a relatively better mood.

But his condition was not stable. Sometimes he missed his son badly. Although he did not say anything about that, I could feel that he regretted having a child and was feeling ashamed of it. One day he said that he heard his son was playing violent computer games that dealt with virtual wars and crimes. And the other day he was concerned that his son would not learn the English language truly and ever read Dickens, Hemingway, and Rousseau.

I had not heard from Mr. B for a few months until one day Mr. K called me in a state to ask if I could call Mr. B. The issue was that Mr. B had got one of the scam phone calls made in the name of the tax department or the court, etc. by fraudulent people, and had believed it. Mr. B had taken that call seriously and had spoken about an imaginary case in a fake court with someone on the other end of the line. It sounds funny because Mr. B had been trying to clarify the reason for his case without any success. He was completely confused, scared and helpless in the hands of that heartless scammer. After that hellish event, Mr. B stopped answering phone calls. He stopped going to work.

He was even scared to leave his house. He believed he would soon be arrested. When I went to his door to help him alleviate his stress, he muttered hastily and fearfully:

"Go, don't stay here, they might arrest you too. No one should know that I have any sort of relationship with anyone...! Go!"

TIC-TAC-TOE

Once I was told that the value of your writing depends on the level of risk you take for it. You, the man who is seated at the corner table of this eatery and focused on reading, even making little notes in the margins of your book, you may not know me. But I have seen you sometimes in this eatery close to the Eglinton subway station. Since you seemed to me very engaged with your reading, I am asking you this question. Have you ever been trapped with no chance to get released? I won't say you are not bold enough to take such risks. But let me tell you a story that probably looks familiar to you. As two unacquainted people, certainly what I am talking about has nothing to do with what you may or may not remember.

Assume you were in an eatery that many people went to after work to get some refreshment or something for dinner – and you can assume, too, that it was close to the Eglinton subway station – on a cold snowy afternoon with a few people taking their coffee after work or seated at the tables and talking together, you were pretending that you were so involved in your book that you weren't listening to other people.

There were three ladies seated around a table beside yours. One of the ladies was from Tanzania, and she had been recently divorced, trying to show herself free, happy, and satisfied. Another lady was from Iran and seemed unhappy with her marriage but obliged to show herself dedicated. And the third one was a lady from Ukraine, who looked happy but thoughtful and hesitant, too. I assume you were sipping your coffee.

The lady from Tanzania turned to the Lady from Iran and said, "So, why you don't go for divorce?" The lady from Ukraine stopped eating and I guess you –I mean someone who I assume was you or your replica - stopped sipping his coffee too. Then the lady from Iran asked, "If I do so, what will be happening after that?" And the lady from Ukraine continued her eating again.

Well, you might become stressed and unhappy with what I am saying now. But let me be honest with you, I won't be intrusive, and I am not a therapist or anything like that. You could assume me as an ordinary friend only. So, you shouldn't be worried if I talk about some of your personal life and feelings.

I know that you have been taught since childhood that it is a sin and ruins your virtue if you have relationship with someone of the opposite sex before marriage. This command made you stressed and agitated after puberty when what you have read in many mystical books and have heard from the folkloric stories and songs was mostly about love. Then you started reading philosophical books to solve this contradiction in your mind.

I'm not sure if those philosophical books helped you or not. But certainly, I can say you learned a lot even though at the same time more contradictions arose in your mind. However, these things could happen to anyone, and I don't like to bother you with such details. What I want to talk about is something that happened and hurt you in the last two or three years. You fell in love from afar with a lady who was your coworker. You were in love with her for sure, but I am not sure if she had the same feeling as you had, or she was expecting more intimacy and closer relationship before a real love can happen. I think that was her mindset about love, and yours was that two individuals can suddenly fall in love just by beholding each other, like what we have read in the old love stories.

You were hesitant to date her, or experience deeper friendship. You were watching her – secretly– when you both were working in the same shift. You had assumed that she does the same thing with similar feelings. You were trying to talk to her. And the funny thing was when you offered her a couple of books from your collection as a gift. You invited her to some concerts and movies. You also joined some gatherings that she was attending with people she knew, like her old classmates, family friends, and others.

I am not going to be dramatic or talk about a tragic love, but it seems that you finally failed in this love. It was an unrequited love.

Long story short, your love ended up with a note that you left for her in the mailbox on a rainy night. If my memory serves correctly, your note was something like this.

"I leave this note in your mailbox because you blocked my cellphone. E & T & C blocked me too. I came to talk to you, forgot you work tonight, but I'm in a rush, so this note is for you.

I'm so sorry, but why did you get mad? – it was a simple joke about abortion. All our friends knew we had never been together. And I believe that you are the purest girl on earth. Still, I love you – and I hope you believe me. We were going to have a picnic that night to have fun. All together. Dammit. E & T & C said jokes make you laugh. I just wanted to be funny, to make you happy, to spice our night.

Tonight, I am going to travel far away. I'll go to my mom's city. Last time I called her, she spoke about euthanasia. She is badly sick. I can't stay here. I'm dead, I'm blocked. You didn't answer my call.

I just heard about a terrible thing that has happened to you. You had an abortion two weeks ago. Trust me, this news hurt me a lot, like the hurt you have felt from this abortion. I failed to understand why it happened to you. I'm very sorry to hear that – very sorry – but remember, I love you. I love you so much."

You did not go far away to another city. You know that your mom passed away some years ago, and you don't have any relatives in this city or the cities around here. The only thing you did was quit your job and that was even more difficult for you. You were jobless for a while till you found another job. You were so stressed that you never paid any real attention to the cheerful details of your surroundings, like the playful kids on their way back from school, or the trees, flowers, rain, or snow in different seasons.

You started smoking cigarettes to calm yourself. But it only made you more frustrated, restless, and sleepless. Then you started taking some pills, and eventually drinking alcohol. But you still did not quit smoking.

Later, you started reading novels like Gustave Flaubert's, *Madame Bovary*, and watching classic love movies.

The moment I am talking about it, in that eatery, you were reading one of those novels. And if you are still agitated with what

I have said so far, please let me tell you one of my memories to make myself clearer.

When I was a schoolboy, our art teacher explained to us how things look smaller as they move away from us. For example, a bird sitting on the branch of a tree near us may be able to cover the trees and a mountain located far distance from our view, but when it flies towards a tree in the distance, it becomes smaller and smaller. Then he put a dot in the upper half of the blackboard with chalk and said this is the dot we see at the furthest point of our gaze. The same thing we call the vanishing point. Then he explained about the horizon line. And he drew a pale line which was the extension of that point. Then he talked about other imaginary lines that reach our eyes like rays of light from objects. He also insisted that the number of these lines is infinite, in fact as the number of objects we may see, and they are even relevant to the angle of our vision looking at the same object. Then he drew other faint and imaginary lines for them. All these hypothetical lines will meet at the vanishing point. He said these lines would merge in such a way that they are no longer distinguishable at all. We, the students, started practicing in our drawing notebooks. I carefully did what the teacher had said. I even used a ruler to draw the lines. And a sharp pencil. So that the lines and dots were very clear and precise like the lines and dots in the math textbook. I was sure that the result of my work was brilliant.

The art teacher would pass by our benches and look at our notebooks and the result of the drawings to give an explanation to each student. When he reached my desk, he paused, looked at my drawing notebook and smiled. He said, "Why have you drawn your imaginary lines so strongly? They are so bold that you cannot erase them. These imaginary lines you have drawn cannot be covered by the objects of your painting. These lines should only exist in your mind. There are no such lines in the real world. You must draw them in such a way that in the end they disappear. Like the wrapping paper of a gift. It will appear at the beginning but will be thrown away soon and be forgotten once you unwrap the gift."

I looked at my teacher and listened to his words because I was perplexed and confused. I was not able to draw imaginary lines that don't really exist in such a way that they could not be seen at all or be erased soon after they are drawn. And imagining throwing away some parts of a gift made me even more puzzled.

The truth is that her body was not able to handle the pregnancy. I don't know if she was smoking or taking pills and alcohol or not.

By the way, at this very moment the three ladies in the eatery started to collect their belongings to leave.

One of the ladies looks at you as she stands up from the table. Although she worked hard on the night shift to get a better income, still she had many struggles with her bills and her body and her unfulfilling life. But she was helpful at work, very friendly with her neighbors, with a real attention to the cheerful details of her surroundings, like the playful kids in their way back from the school, or the trees, flowers, rain, or snow in different seasons.

On the days she came to the eatery she could see a man seated in the corner reading and writing in the margins of his book. She had a feeling that he would be an amiable man. A very good, knowledgeable, and caring man.

Today she was unwell and seemed to be a little out of energy. She had a terrible situation in the hospital a few weeks ago. She came very close to losing her ability to be a mother forever. Thankfully she survived the surgery, but she lost her baby in the second or third month of her pregnancy. Behind her smiles and hard work still the counting of that nurse in the hospital echoes in her mind. The nurse on her right side smiled and she felt a needle in her left hand. Then the nurse on her left side smiled and started counting, one, two, three…

Yes, she is good now, she survived, she left the recovery room a few weeks ago, and now she is about to leave the eatery. Probably she glances again at the man who is overwhelmed with his reading.

Perhaps, even, she has a feeling like this: *"What if this man leaves the eatery by chance now? What if he comes in the same direction as I go toward the subway station? And what if I slip accidentally when we both walk along the street on this snowy day? Or when we are*

83

going down the stairs of the subway station, my leg twists because of the snow or my body weakness? Then, probably he grabs my arm. He might even be so worried about me; he wants to call 911. But I can convince him that I'm fine and can walk down the stairs just by leaning on his arm."

A BAKERY CALLED "SERENITY"

This bakery was where you found your first job at last. And now, a few months after starting your work here you are kicked out of your job, or, as they say, you are laid off. You don't have the level of experience and knowledge that is normally required for working with computers, or performing a high-quality customer service, manufacturing, or maintenance activities. Therefore, working in that bakery in a small town far from Toronto was the only practical option for you as a thirty-two-year-old Persian woman. You and your husband immigrated to Canada about two years ago.

In Iran, your husband used to work in a bank, and you were a high school graduated girl. It was a situation very pleasing to both your and your husband's families. And probably that was why both families were confident about your marriage. You started a lovely life. Your husband was responsible for the living costs, and you were responsible for the housekeeping.

In fact, what you learned from your kind and patient mother helped you a lot to find your first job at this bakery. You have learned many things from your mother, like how a teaspoon of sugar is needed in addition to salt to make a good dough. Or how being silent and patient is necessary for a decent girl. Unfortunately, before you and your husband came to Canada you had two miscarriages. Of course, that was not the only reason for moving to Canada, but it was also discussed too when you and your husband were talking to each other about how to improve your lifestyle through immigration. Your husband hoped to find a better job in a bank in Canada. And you were hopeful of receiving better health services during your next pregnancy.

Your husband moved from one job to another during the first year of your immigration and your little savings shrunk and shrunk. It was a very despairing time. Your husband started showing his nervousness, and you tried hard to find a job. Eventually, you found one, then you and your husband moved to this town together and rented a basement apartment at the other end of this street on which the bakery called "Serenity" is located.

At the beginning the word "serenity" seemed exciting to you. It seemed like a good omen. In the bakery, during the first week, while you were being trained by your mentor, who was another lady almost your age, you learned how to move the pallets, how to carry the bags of flour, and how to dump the garbage bins into the dumpsters outside of the bakery shop.

You also learned about the exciting history of your workplace. The owner of the bakery, a middle-aged woman, explained that the yeast they used had been touched or blessed by a saint many years ago, and that is why many people came from faraway places to buy their bread. The owner was a calm but determined middle-aged lady who never shouted, and she worked all day before any of the other workers started their job, and into the night after all the workers had left the bakery. She always wore an apron and covered her head with a black and soft hair net that all workers must pull over their hair. The owner moved from one side of the bakery to the other to supervise all activities. Sometimes she worked as a cashier, too, or arranged with the suppliers for the next deliveries.

You don't remember the name of that saint who blessed the yeast many years or many decades ago. In fact, you are not even sure if you learned that name at all. You know why – because your ears were not able to absorb the words of a new language, and the sounds of unfamiliar accents properly. At the beginning you thought that you had a hearing problem. But soon you understood that familiarity with sounds and images are important to our brain in the processing of what we hear and see. Once your brain had been moved out of its habitual patterns, you felt that you were replaced with a very weak person who is unable to feel smart. And it was too painful and disturbing for you to ask people again and again to repeat what they had told you just minutes before.

Today, once you entered the bakery and before you even change your clothes, the owner politely called you to come by the cashier and she nicely paid your salary and told you that she cannot tolerate temptation of her costumers at all, it certainly ruins the reputation of her bakery. And she added that it is ok if you want to use her bakery as a reference for your next job. During her conversation with you, her tone remained unchanged and calm as always. Then she left the place to look after her daily duties.

And during the time that you were talking desperately and confused with the owner of the bakery, your mentor was standing up close to a small door that separates the store from the bakery behind it watching you silently and angrily.

You were shocked, very shocked, because you failed to understand why she fired you. You were shaking with worry and anger. You were not even able to put your words in your mind properly. But eventually you asked, "Why? What have I done wrong?" I understand that you were not able to communicate appropriately at that time.

Once the owner left to supervise her business, your mentor said many things about yesterday when Alex had come to your place to help you to buy a used washer and dryer for your basement apartment. You just comprehended that your mentor talked about "prostitution" and it's an illegal thing. You remember that she said, "Police might arrest you because of prostitution." And she left you there and came back to continue her work at the bakery too. You were alone. There was not even one customer in the store at that time.

You left the bakery with your salary in your pocket. It was a cold early December. In the street suddenly you started crying. You had been shaking and crying involuntarily. All the memories of your last month were flowing into your mind as your tears were running from your eyes.

Your husband had left you to work with a wealthy Iranian man who had promised him a good income. But you suspected that your husband wanted to leave you to go after a girlfriend, while working for that wealthy man sounds like monkey business to you. You learned the phrase "monkey business" as an idiom for illegal work from the husband of your landlord.

One day when you had been upstairs to use the shared washer and dryer of the house, the husband of your landlord used "monkey business" to express what he thought about the job that your husband is involved with. The shared washer and dryer are located on the main floor of the building, and you were upstairs to wash your clothes then you saw the husband of landlord doing something in the kitchen. When the landlord, who is a middle-aged lady, came back home, she seemed very angry. She shouted, "Why are you coming to use the washer and dryer when I'm not home? Why are you talking to my husband privately? Why have you paid last month's rent to my husband when I am the landlord?" In fact, you didn't see any difference between paying your rent to the landlord herself or to her husband. Your mother used to say that her husband takes better care of their money.

And moreover, landlord said that she had rented the basement apartment to your husband and not to you, so you should leave at the end of the month.

Then, yesterday, when your mentor was on vacation, Alex came to the bakery. Alex is a young handy man who comes to the bakery regularly. He buys bread and biscuits and sometimes he fixes the equipment of the bakery too. In the bakery, Alex talks to your mentor in the English that you do not know any word of. He talks to the owner of the bakery and the other people. Sometimes Alex and your mentor joke and laugh too.

Yesterday, when your mentor was on vacation, and you were working as the cashier, Alex came to buy bread. You told him that you wanted to purchase and install a washer and dryer for your basement apartment. You were assuming that if you pay for a washer and dryer, it would be considered as a treat by your landlord and would make her happy. You were hoping it would help you to reconcile with your landlord. In fact, the husband of your landlord had given you this idea. Sometimes, he spoke to you a few words secretly, like when you were about to leave the apartment, or when you and he were both carrying the garbage bins to the sidewalk. After the landlord told you that you should leave her house soon, her husband brought you this idea that if you pay for a washer and dryer, it would be beneficial for both landlord and tenant. And it might help you to reconcile.

So, you asked Alex about purchasing a washer and dryer, and Alex told you that he knows a good used washing machine that can be bought at a reasonable price. But to ensure a smooth and easy installation, he needed to measure the place and inspect the availability of water pipes, sewage system, and electricity.

Then, last night after your work, Alex came to your apartment and while he was doing the measurements and inspection, you ran to make a well-brewed Persian tea for him to thank him for his effort.

While Alex was explaining the connection of water pipes to you, when you were in the washroom together, the landlord appeared at the top of the stairs staring angrily at you both. The door of the basement apartment was wide open because, like the other decent things that you have learned from your mother, it is your habit to leave the door open when you are alone in a room with another man who is not your husband.

The landlord shouted at you and Alex while moving her hands and kicking the stairs. Alex tried to talk to the landlord in the language that you did not know any word of. The landlord replied to Alex with the same language and at the end she pointed to the exit of the house and repeated some words just as angrily as before. Alex left the house immediately. I am not sure, but apparently the landlord had called the owner of the bakery or your mentor last night.

And today, while you were crying heavily, without knowing what you must do, you crossed the street and walked along. In the front of a motel not too far from the bakery a young lady was sipping her coffee. You remembered the motel and the young lady as well. Because it's the place that you had rented a room for a few days once you and your husband had moved to this town. The nice girl who was sipping her coffee recognized you too, because you had a short and sweet conversation with this girl every day during your residence. She was the one who taught you how to use captions when you watch TV, and how turning on the captions helps you to increase your comprehension.

She was Amanda, an Indigenous girl, who works in this motel as a receptionist, and is the student of paralegal studies in a college in the adjacent town. Amanda invited you to come to the lobby. She gave you some napkins to clean the tears from your face. She prepared you a coffee. She sat beside you on the sofa. She asked you, "What happened?" and you explained everything hastily without even concentrating on your words. To tell the truth, you had been very disturbed and distracted. But when you repeated what your mentor had told you an hour ago, you started crying and shaking again. You hated to repeat the word "prostitution."

Amanda kindly tried to calm you. And even she helped you laugh by saying, "Like you, I always love to use the present tense verbs in my sentences. To be honest, I use present tense verbs most of the time. But it could be confusing for other people." She was kindly speaking slowly, without using unfamiliar phrases and terms. She was also repeating her sentences to ensure you understood her. Then she continued, "Don't worry. No worries at all. You have not done anything illegal. Now, it's better you go back to your house. Stay there and take a rest for a few hours. I will come to meet you after my work." She smiled and continued, "I have a Mini-Van. If you need to move to another place, I can help you. Don't worry. Soon you will find a better job, and a better place to live. But of course, I will help you to talk to your landlord and the owner of the bakery first."

"And," Amanda continued when you were about to leave the motel, she looked at your running shoes that became wet after your wandering along the street and said, "I think you need a pair of snow boots, too."

NEW YORK CITY

On her way back to Toronto from New York City, she was tired, but still, she did not want to close her eyes lest she miss anything spectacular. She had spent three nights and four days on a short tourist trip late that summer. It was her first trip out of Canada after she arrived in Toronto a few years ago. She had planned this trip herself. She was educated enough to check the websites, buy a bus ticket, find a hotel, book the events etc. for her three nights and four days travel to New York.

She was an Iranian girl who had finished her B.Sc. in Microbiology from a university in Iran about ten years ago. She had refused to get married and, although her marriage was the major concern of her parents, she had always insisted in response that she was determined to migrate to North America or Europe. And whenever her parents or someone else said, "Why you don't marry someone who also wants to immigrate?" she would respond, "No, this means marriage for the sake of immigration. It means selling both my heart and my freedom. I need both for a successful immigration. Also, I don't know how immigration will be going on when it is chained with marriage."

From childhood, she was always a good reader of books. Children books when she was in elementary school and later when she entered high school started reading many masterpieces like the works of Hemingway, Steinbeck, Fitzgerald, and other novelists, playwrights, and poets. When she was a university student, she had watched many brilliant movies from Iranian or other filmmakers. She had been fond of good music too, whether Persian music or western music.

As so it was obvious that she had learned about the famous Iranian actors, writers, and musicians who have been successful in their carriers after their migration to Europe or North America. And that was her incentive to seek the same success when she migrated to Canada.

She had spent several months as a volunteer in a community center, then in a school in Toronto. Then she had found a basic job not relevant to her education. She moved to a better job after a year, and then moved to her current job in the suburbs of Toronto. A job still not relevant to her education but with a better hourly rate.

Meanwhile, she had some hangouts with some Persian friends and some friends from different communities, too. Sometimes some young men were interested in a permanent relationship with her. But she could not see any difference between such relationships and those relationships that her parents were encouraging her to have before her immigration. Therefore, she was not interested in such friendships and none of them had been continued more than two or three simple hangouts.

And finally, when she obtained her citizenship and her Canadian passport, she decided to go to a trip. She had a little saved after all. Her savings were encouraging her to plan a visit to New York City to see Broadway and the Statue of Liberty.

On her way back to Toronto in the bus, a forty-some years-old man had been seated next to her. Her seat was by the bus window, and she had been quietly looking at everything like buildings, streets, trees… all the time and had paid no attention to her neighbor or other passengers.

After two or three hours, the bus stopped at a small plaza for a short washroom and coffee break.

She and the man seated next to her, each a cup of coffee in hand, were standing lose to the bus waiting for the driver to call all passengers. Still, she was paying no attention to the man beside her.

The man said, "Nice weather" demanding some attention.

She glanced at the man with a smile, "Yes, it's very nice".

At first glance, he seemed like a white Canadian man. But his accent, although he was speaking English fluently – as she heard him when he was talking to others – was different than what she had heard from Canadian English speakers. For instance, he was stressing "s" like "z". Then the man extended his desire for conversation with more questions, "Have you been on a business trip to New York?"

"No. Just a vacation. And you?"

"Oh, I see. No, I was on a business trip. But why didn't you go to other cities like Las Vegas, or Chicago?"

"I just wanted to visit the Statue of Liberty and Broadway."

"Yes, very famous places. I'm sure you have visited the Statue of Liberty, but I'm interested to know what show you watched in Broadway."

"Nothing. I couldn't find any of my favorites."

"What are your favorite shows? I'm surprised that you have not found anything attractive on Broadway."

"My favorites are masterpieces, like the plays written by Tennessee Williams, Edward Albee, or Eugene O'Neill."

"Oh, who are they? I've never heard of them." And he laughed as if he had told a very funny joke.

"Well, they have been the foremost American dramatists, like Hemingway. I hope you have heard of Hemingway at least."

"Yes, of course. Once I started reading "The Old Man and The Sea" Ernest Hemingway in high school, but I didn't finish it." Then laughed again as if he had told another very funny joke.

Probably he had expected the same reaction from his fellow traveler too. Since he didn't hear any laugh in response, he changed his mood and continued asking his questions, "So, probably you like classics. Don't you like modern movies at all?"

"What modern movies?"

"There are many modern popular ones. About aliens, dinosaurs, spaceships, and stuff like that. Have you watched any of them?"

"I know what you are talking about. But I can watch such things on my cellphone though. I don't need to go to Broadway to watch them. I went to New York to watch what has made New York New York."

"Well, what is making New York New York is still on the scenes and screens. They even make thousands of times more than those you talked about. Those you pointed to were living and working probably a hundred years ago. Well, now things have changed. Lives have changed. And tastes have changed too. That's how the market works. If the filmmakers still want to show the countryside, then they will go bankrupt soon. You like to live in countryside I guess."

"I don't know how you relate the great dramatists to the countryside. What I'm still interested to know is if still anybody work like Eugene O'Neill for instance."

"Well, there should be some writers like him. I believe there are."

"But I didn't see any."

"Where have you looked for them?"

She became puzzled by this response because she had not thought about that before. And had thought instead that Broadway is the best place to look for masterpieces, and now she felt unsure. To escape from this question she asked instead, "What is the field of your business?"

"Advertisement."

"Which company are you working for?"

"I used to work for some big companies. Companies with two thousand plus workers. Now I am running my own business."

"Good for you. What is the name of your company?"

"Well, it is still under development. My website is under construction. But I have started hiring people though."

"Hiring employees? Sounds you run a very successful business."

"It is indeed. In this business or any business, you just need to know people. I know people very well. Also, you need to know the language of art. And I know art perfectly."

"But you said you have left "The Old Man and The Sea" unfinished," and laughed sardonically. The man said, "No. Don't get me wrong. You are obsessed with iconic figures. But art is different. Art is everything that can absorb people and help people to pay money for their happiness. Do you have any objection?"

"Well, what I don't understand is how do you connect what people pay for something, I mean in general, to art?"

"Hummm! You're smart…That's the "know-how" of my business. I'm normally not supposed to talk about the secrets of my job to everybody. But I will open a bit of it to you. See, there are two groups of people. Young and old. You might think of age only when we talk about young and old. But that's not true. Young and old people are not divided by age only. Some young people could be included in the group of old people, like you as a young person who is obsessed with old plays. And there are many old people who, actually, belong to the group of young people. And I can say there are many more such people than you might imagine. The trick is knowing that young people care more about playing with toys. They enjoy the play and leave the toys and forget them after a while and look for new toys to play with. On the other side there are old people who care more about toys and less about playing with toys."

She became perplexed again. Her mind was engaged in a challenge with what she had heard. Then the man smiled and said, "I would like to offer you a job."

"But you don't have a company yet."

"I do have it. I have a lot of experience in the field of advertisement."

"So, what is the job?"

"You can work as a model for my company."

"A model?"

"Yes. You are obsessed with icons. That means you want to become a famous person, like an actor. Working as a model for my company will make you famous. It's the best venue for your success. For sure."

"Famous? Through flyers for toys?"

"Yes flyers. There is nothing wrong with flyers. Those are what people need and read them in their daily lives, perhaps even more than books. And no, the advertisements are not only for toys. There could be toys and other things that people are interested about, like, jewelry, cosmetics, dresses, and underwear."

She looked at this offer indifferently, while the man had been expecting an exited like, *"Wow. Oh my gosh…are you serious… that's so exciting!"* Her reaction was very disappointing.

The conversation ended at this point. The bus was about to leave, and she boarded with the man and the other passengers.

During the rest of the trip, they neither talked about avant-garde writers nor about advertisements. The man had been either silently scrolling in his cellphone, or napping. And she was thinking about a question that her fellow traveler had asked her, *"Where have you looked for them?"*

Also, she spent the rest of her trip wandering in what she had read already about the different groups of people and their different approaches to a meaningful life.

Finally, they arrived at the last station of the bus in Toronto, and they had to leave the bus, grab their luggage, and go on their own way home. When they had grabbed their luggage and had been about to say goodbye, the man bent a little to her and said with a low voice, "I thought a little more, I don't think that working as a model would be a right choice for you at all. A model should start working at a younger age to have a successful career. Enjoy the rest of your day."

A REPEATING ALARM TONE

Your "Best wishes" email bounced back with an autoreply, the email that you sent to a close co-worker after he announced his retirement and his last day of work. You had both been working in the same office for a few years in Toronto. But recently you moved to another building. Still, you thought that you should send him your best wishes with your gratitude in response to his kind and valuable help during that period when you were in the same office as co-workers. However, your email bounced back with a common autoreply that said if you have any urgent issues with this subject, send your email to this person and if you have any urgent issues with that subject send your email to that person. But you did not have any urgent issue with this or that subject. Your urgent issue was about his feelings. You wanted to ask him how he felt today. You wanted to remind him that he is not alone. You understood that although your co-workers in the last few days had sent him some congratulations and heartwarming words or flourish emojis, or had even gone a step further and imagined him lying on a warm sandy beach with a cold drink in hand, you had known very well how difficult it would be to spend that few minutes in the elevator for the last time when a retiree goes down to the lobby and leaves the building. You knew that even if (just if) your former co-worker came tomorrow to see his friends, that he shouldn't be surprised if his access to the building was deactivated, and he would be just an unknown person there. So, your feelings are as useless as the auto-reply email. The check mark beside his name in the system has been changed to a cross, and he has become a stranger.

How did you know that it would be a very hard moment when he leaves the building? You saw that situation a few years ago at a gathering for another co-worker who was leaving the office. That day she retired too. Now you remember when you saw her for the first time. When you first came to that building.

She was working at the small reception counter, her realm. On her motorized wheelchair, she was helpful – and fast like a race car driver. Calling the offices, taking your documents, connecting you to the important places, working with the fax machine and copier, speaking to people to arrange everything for you as a beginner. Also, she decorated the lobby for the New Year's holidays every year, very happily and enthusiastically. Quite fascinating, admirable.

One day it was her turn to retire. In her retirement gathering in one of the board rooms of the office, we had cake and coffee; we signed the card with our best wishes. Even one of the senior managers gave her a camera because he knew that she was very fond of traveling and taking photos. All had been arranged: face to face appreciations, smiles, and good things to eat and drink. All the civilities had been maintained.

After that gathering you were going to leave the office early that day. After that retirement meeting, you and she were the only travelers in that familiar elevator that you had used to start and end your working days for some years. When you were about to leave the office, everyone was still at their desks, except you two. You and that retired lady.

In the elevator, you saw her pressing her lips together and squeezing her hands around the box of that camera. When you both reached the lobby, you saw that she was crying silently. The lobby had two doors on the opposite sides of the building. You were going to exit the north door because it was closer to your car, but you followed her to the south door. She was hyperventilating, and for a few seconds you felt that you would have to call 911. But you saw a wheelchair accessible bus ready to drive her home. And the ramp of that bus was lowering with a repeating alarm tone.

ABOUT THE AUTHOR

Mansour Noorbakhsh writes and translates poems in both English and his first language, Farsi. In his writings, he tries to be a voice for freedom, human rights, and the environment. He believes a dialogue between people everywhere is an essential need for developing a peaceful world, and poetry can play an important part in this dialogue. As part of this project to build bridges between the Persian people and Canadian communities and culture he presents the work of contemporary Canadian poets – both in English and with translations into Farsi – on the weekly Persian radio program *Namaashoum* (https://persianradio. net/poets/ or https://t.me/ottawaradio).

Mansour has published the following two books, and several articles and poems in Farsi.

به سراغ من اگر می آیید / زندگی وشعر سهراب سپهری

The Life and Poetry of Sohrab Sepehri

دیدار با فلق / زندگی و شعر منوچهر آتشی

The Life and Poetry of Manuchehr Atashi

Mansour's other works include his poem in English, "In Search of Shared Wishes" which was published in 2017, as well as poems published in "WordCity, (https://wordcitylit.ca)", and several anthologies.

Mansour now lives with his wife and their two children in Toronto, Canada.